ENORMOUSLY
PUZZLED

THE PUZZLED MYSTERY ADVENTURE SERIES: BOOK 5

P.J. Nichols

Paperback ISBN 978-4-910091-20-4
Hardcover ISBN 978-4-910091-22-8

pjnichols.com

Cover design by Thomas Paehler

For all the frontline workers,
Your dedication to helping the world battle
the COVID-19 pandemic, and the risks you
take while doing your jobs, make you all true
heroes.

CHAPTER 1

"Peter," the banquet hall manager coldly told him. "Pots and pans."

"Again?" Peter complained. "I washed the pots and pans last Saturday. And the Saturday before that. It's gotta be someone else's turn today."

Wayne—the owner, manager, and head chef of the cheapest banquet hall in town—didn't care enough about Peter's dissatisfaction to reply; he simply pointed to the giant sink in the corner of the kitchen and strolled toward his comfortable office.

"Jerk," Peter mumbled under his breath after Wayne closed the door.

"Bad luck, dude," Peter's friend Michael told him. "Looks like he's got it in for you."

"This is just Wayne's sick little way of getting revenge on Brad," Peter said.

* * *

Three years back, Bradley had (very briefly) worked at the banquet hall. And his tenure there had turned into folklore.

Bradley had started in early October of his second year of high school. (Since the banquet hall had a reputation for being one of the crappiest places to work, that meant people quit frequently, so they were always hiring.)

During his fifth shift, Bradley had been given the duty of scrubbing all the pots and pans—by far the worst of the post-dinner tasks—for the third consecutive Saturday. He didn't complain, he just robotically went to the back corner of the kitchen and got to work.

But after close to two hours of mindlessly scraping and scrubbing (and having barely even made a dent in the pile), boredom got the better of him.

Bradley turned off the water, put the ratty, old scrubbing sponge on the edge of the sink, and walked to his boss' office door.

He knocked loudly a few times, as he figured Wayne had probably dozed off. When his grumpy boss yelled, "Yeah! What?" Bradley entered the office and told Wayne something that was now considered to be *legendary.*

Bradley began by calmly explaining that he thought it would be in the best interest of the business to invest in bigger and deeper sinks.

All Wayne did was grunt out an irritated, "Why? What for? That'd cost a fortune."

Bradley told him that if they had big enough

sinks, then whoever used them would be able to "get right in and be at one with the beloved pots!"

Wayne (using some very rude words) told Bradley exactly what he thought of this sarcastic remark.

* * *

"Brad rattled his chains a little with that sink remark," Peter said to Michael, "but it was when he pulled a no-show on New Year's Eve that Wayne went berserk."

"But doesn't everyone have to work on New Year's?" Michael asked.

"Brad goes by his own set of rules," Peter replied. "He had gone and talked to Wayne in early December, and said he couldn't work on New Year's Eve because he was going to a party. Wayne then apparently told Brad, 'Either come that night or don't bother coming back.'"

"He was just on a power trip," Michael commented. "He wouldn't really fire anyone. He can barely keep this place staffed as it is."

"Wayne didn't have the opportunity to fire Brad," Peter went on, "because Brad phoned in fifteen minutes before his New Year's Eve shift was supposed to start, and quit."

"Pete," Michael whispered suddenly. "Shh… Wayne's coming this way."

"Peter!" Wayne hollered out. "What part of the word *pots and pans* did you not understand?"

"Words," Peter whispered to himself. "Pots and

pans are *three words,* not *a word."*

Peter had always been the kind of kid who covered his tracks, and today was no exception: He put down the four dirty wine glasses he was holding.

"Someone put a bunch of wine glasses over by the pots," he expressionlessly said. "You should be thanking me for not breaking them instead of yelling at me."

Although Wayne wanted to snap at Peter, he couldn't argue with that comment: Broken wine glasses would have meant a little less profit for him.

Peter then slowly made his way back to the massive mountain of dirty pots and trays.

"There's gotta be a million better ways to earn minimum wage," he mumbled to himself while twisting on the hot water.

* * *

Peter knew he had at least four hours of "solitary confinement" here at the sink: a length of time that would certainly affect anyone's mental health. In an attempt to maintain his sanity, he decided that while his hands were doing the cleaning, he would get his mind focused on something else.

"Pots and pans," he said softly. "P.O.T.S. A.N.D. P.A.N.S... I wonder how many words I can spell with those letters?"

* * *

It wasn't long before he lost count of *how many,* but his photographic memory certainly didn't forget any of the words he had already said. He was currently working on five-letter ones, having already rattled off everything shorter.

"Stand," he said to himself. "Panda, spats..."

* * *

That little game managed to make the first twenty minutes of scrubbing somewhat bearable. But before he knew it, the disorganized mess of dishes was still staring at him, almost taunting him. (Now he kind of understood why Bradley wanted to swim with the pots: At least that would inject a tad of fun into this mindless and mundane work...)

CHAPTER 2

"Dude, wake up," Bradley said loudly while shaking Peter back and forth.

Peter was exactly where he was supposed to be—in bed—but considering he hadn't gotten home until nearly midnight, he definitely didn't need to be forcefully woken up by his elder brother at six fifteen in the morning.

"It's Sunday, man," Peter grunted. "Leave me alone."

Bradley switched on Peter's bedroom light and sat down at his brother's desk.

"Pete, I gotta tell you something important," he said. "Well, I don't really *want* to tell you this, I feel obligated."

"What are you talking about?" Peter asked, still half asleep.

Bradley yanked the blanket off Peter.

"Come on, listen up," he instructed his brother. "It's about Nik."

Peter sat up ramrod straight.

"What happened?" he asked. "Is she okay?"

"Yeah, calm down," Bradley told him. "She didn't have an accident or anything like that."

"Then what is so important," Peter questioned his brother, "that you felt it necessary to wake me up the morning after I scrubbed Wayne's stupid pots for close to five hours?"

"Nik worked last night too, right?" Bradley asked quite directly. "At the restaurant she's been at for ages?"

"Yeah," Peter replied. "She did the three-to-nine shift, which is the busiest one. I hope she got some big tips."

"Okay, Pete," Bradley said, expression very serious. "There's no way to say this nicely: Your girlfriend went out for coffee with some tall dude last night."

"Nice try," Peter said back. "Where did you hide the camera in here to catch my reaction?"

Bradley didn't flinch.

"Pete, I'm not lying," he explained. "My buddy Tom works at the coffee shop she showed up at. He saw her come in at a quarter past nine, and leave when it closed at ten. Tom recognized her right away, but since he works in the back, she never saw him."

"And let me guess," Peter said sarcastically, "he phoned and told you all this last night?"

"Yes," Bradley replied right away. "Anyway, look, I didn't come in here to argue with you. I'm just giving you the facts."

Bradley then stood up, switched off the light, and got ready to leave. "I've got track practice, so I've gotta go," he said. "If you don't believe me, phone Tom and ask him yourself. I wrote his number on the pad of paper here."

Peter grabbed his sheets and got comfortable again. What a bunch of balderdash! Nicola would never do something like that.

Peter's eyes were closed, but he certainly wasn't going to be able to trick himself into sleeping again. (He would be obsessing over this until he got confirmation that Bradley had been making it all up...)

CHAPTER 3

"Morning, Mr. Sleepyhead," Peter's mom said when he finally came down to eat breakfast at a little past eight o'clock.

"Hey," Peter replied.

He had just spent the last two hours lying in bed—ruminating over each and every minute he had spent with Nicola over the past couple of weeks—hoping to figure out when (or if) his girlfriend had been acting odd.

"How's the leg doing?" his mom asked.

"Still gets a little sore when I have to stand for hours on end," he answered. "But the doc said that would improve on its own over time, right?"

About four and a half months had passed since Peter had broken his ankle. The cast was long since a thing of the past, plus he had completed his final physiotherapy session about two weeks ago. Therefore, all he could do now was just wait for Mother Nature to do her work.

* * *

Peter was doing a pretty good job (so far) this year of sticking to the New Year's Resolution he had set for himself.

(No, his New Year's Resolution was not to worry less, as that would have been way too big to tackle!)

Peter had decided the best way to defeat his "worry gremlins" was to sneak up on them in ways they wouldn't expect. On January 1, he had started with his first baby step, which was to break his unnecessary habit of eating the same breakfast every single day.

That meant Peter's days of cornflakes and pulp-free orange juice were now finished. And contrary to his worry that this change to toast (or waffles, or pancakes, or last night's leftovers) would upset his digestive system, his stomach had had no issues at all.

His parents had, of course, noticed what Peter was doing, but elected to never comment on it.

Today, Peter was preparing himself a peanut butter and banana sandwich, something he decided to try as an experiment for lunch about a month or so ago. (He loved peanut butter, and bananas, so why not?)

"Oh, Pete, I almost forgot," his mom said as she poured herself another tall mug of decaf. "The elderly man you meet up with at the community center, Mr. Winchester, called here last night."

Peter just about choked on his mouthful of high glycemic index food. He quickly grabbed his grapefruit juice—another change to his breakfast routine—and swallowed two big gulps.

"Wh.. what did you say?" he asked, unable to mask the terror in his voice.

"Oh, not to worry," his mom answered. "He's fine. He just said he's having an out-of-town guest over next weekend, so he needs to cancel next week's meet-up at the community center."

Thankfully, Peter's mom was already heading back to the living room when she said that, and therefore she didn't see all the color drain out of her son's face.

"This is bad," Peter said quietly, leaving the rest of his breakfast on the kitchen table and dashing upstairs. "Very, very bad."

CHAPTER 4

Three months ago, Mr. Winchester realized he needed a way to be able to let Peter know quickly when there was new and pertinent news regarding Xavier, and the method they had settled on was for Mr. Winchester to phone and say he couldn't make their next planned meeting. (Was Xavier already here? Or had Torin, their informant who had infiltrated Xavier's group, been discovered?)

Peter's "worry meter" was off the scales as his shaky hand reached for the phone.

* * *

"Good morning, Peter," Mr. Winchester said when he picked up the phone. "I see you received my message."

"Yeah," Peter answered, voice cracking because he was so worried. "What's going on? Is Xavier on Earth?"

"Oh, Peter," his elderly friend responded rather casually. "No, no. Nothing like that."

Peter let out a huge sigh of relief. "Okay, I'll be right over," he said, not even waiting for Mr. Winchester to say good-bye before he hung up.

* * *

He dressed and took Bradley's new road bike—not caring if Bradley yelled at him later for borrowing it without asking—as he needed to get to Mr. Winchester's house ASAP.

* * *

Peter didn't even bother knocking when he arrived; He just walked right in (while huffing and puffing like crazy) and said, "Okay, let's hear it. What's going on?"

"Peter, are you alright?" Zoltan's mother, Sapphire, said to their red-faced and profusely sweaty teenage guest. "Let me get you some water."

"Peter," Mr. Winchester said from his rocking chair. "Didn't your therapist tell you to be careful about jumping to conclusions? You know how that can start the anxiety spiral."

(Peter was unimpressed that everyone suddenly understood more about his mental health challenges than he did...)

"Have a seat, Peter," Zoltan's father, Demetrius, said very calmly. "We will start explaining things while my lovely wife gets you that water. And before you ask: No, Xavier is

NOT on his way here."

"Thank goodness," Peter said between breaths.

"I received a communique from my nephew Torin last night," Demetrius began. "As you are well aware, he hadn't sent one in weeks, and we were all beginning to worry that Xavier might have figured out Torin was a spy. Luckily, that's not the case."

"Then what did he say?" Peter asked.

"It was a fairly short message," Zoltan told Peter while sitting down beside him. "Plus, it was somewhat vague time-wise. It said that Xavier had amassed an army of over one hundred weather gods, and that they were contemplating a date, likely a couple months down the road, for a mass invasion of Earth."

"But I thought he had *thousands* of followers," Peter mentioned. "Why would that number suddenly drop to a *hundred?*"

"His supporters do indeed still number in the thousands," Zoltan explained. "The majority of them are just average citizens, though."

"Oh, I see," Peter said. "So about a hundred are trained weather gods... But isn't a hundred, like, a lot?"

"It would appear," Mr. Winchester commented, "that Xavier has a big enough force that he thinks he can't lose. And all they have left to do now is coordinate the specifics of their mission to come here and steal the amulet."

"But," Peter said, finally able to breathe normally again. "But how can we get ready for what's coming if we don't know what's coming?" (That question didn't make much sense, did it?)

"I've only had a single night to think this over," Mr. Winchester said, "but one thing is certain: We need help."

"Help?" Peter asked.

"Supernatural help," Mr. Winchester went on. "We may have the amulet, which is a huge plus, but Zoltan can only be in one place at a time. If Xavier's troops attack multiple locations simultaneously, they could destroy countless cities and kill thousands upon thousands of innocent people."

"But how do we, uh, call for help?" Peter asked. "Communication with Torin is only safe one-way, right? If we try sending a message to him, they would intercept it immediately."

"True," Mr. Winchester replied. "Sapphire, would you care to explain?"

"Peter," Sapphire began. "We have come up with a... uh... plan of sorts. The only way to get a message to Torin is to hand-deliver it. And the only way to hand-deliver one is to use Leonardo's ship, and—"

"But they'd spot the ship on their radar and intercept it the instant it arrived!" Peter said loudly. "Torin would never even see the message."

"Actually," Demetrius told Peter, "Torin was

15

assigned, by Xavier himself, to specifically watch for any signs of us trying to come to Sevlar. He and a couple others would be the ones to intercept our ship."

"But if he's not alone," Peter said, "then others would see the message too, and we'd still be busted."

No one responded to Peter, they just calmly looked at him... with great curiosity.

"I think I get it," Peter said, cracking his first smile of the day. "We are going to hide a secret message within the message, aren't we?"

"That's why I called you last night," Mr. Winchester said. "We certainly can't come up with this on our own."

"But who's going to actually deliver it?" Peter asked.

"I will," Sapphire answered, rather unexpectedly. "Demetrius needs to be here to help Zoltan, and Leonardo will be coordinating everything."

"How many people do you think Torin can recruit?" Peter asked next. "Fifty? Or maybe a hundred?"

Mr. Winchester giggled a little—which appeared kind of like a nervous laugh—and then replied, "A handful, at most."

"But we wouldn't stand a chance against Xavier's onslaught!" Peter said, shaking his head.

Although that comment had sounded like he

was admitting prematurely to defeat, in fact it was quite the opposite; It was Peter's subconscious way of firing himself up.

"We haven't even begun contemplating how to handle that," Mr. Winchester told him. "We are hoping that *you* can help with the brainstorming."

* * *

Three or four years ago, the pressure Peter constantly put on himself to be perfect would quite regularly cause him to have anxiety or panic attacks. But that was not so much the case anymore. He had proven himself countless times over the past few years, and was confident he could outsmart even the most intelligent adversaries. If anyone could come up with something ideal, it was Peter.

"I'm going to take a walk," he told everyone. "I think better when I'm moving, and alone."

"Of course," Zoltan said, smiling. "Take your time. You know where to find us."

CHAPTER 5

After about ninety minutes of walking back and forth along the seldom-used dirt road near Mr. Winchester's home, Peter had concocted a scheme that was worth pitching to everyone. It wasn't ironclad by any means, but it was the best he could come up with in such a limited amount of time.

"Pancakes are ready!" Zoltan shouted from the front porch. "Get 'em while they're hot!"

Peter was only about thirty or forty meters from the front door, so he eagerly jogged back. (The innovative plan he had thought up still required some tinkering, and the sugar provided by fresh pancakes—and the pool of maple syrup he would pour over them—would certainly keep his creative juices flowing.)

"Smells great," Peter said to Zoltan as he removed his shoes. "Did you guys already eat?"

"Certainly not," Sapphire said from the sofa. "The first set of pancakes have your name on them."

* * *

Explaining his plan while eating seemed like a poor idea, so Peter decided to wait until he was finished his last bite. But he was so anxious to get started that he put back two big pancakes in less than five minutes. (Good thing his mom wasn't here: He would have heard an earful about not vacuuming up his lunch!)

"Please feel free to stop me at any time to ask questions," Peter began. "I probably overlooked a bunch of things. But anyway, here goes. My entire plan is based on the following premise: It would be futile to just sit here and wait for them to arrive. I mean, think about it, even if Torin miraculously found ten or twenty weather gods to help us, we'd still be ridiculously outnumbered."

"What do you propose then?" Demetrius asked.

"We are going to make Xavier think," Peter answered, "that he has a chance to steal the amulet quickly and easily if he comes here right away."

"But we can't prepare anything that fast," Zoltan said. "We need time."

"Oops, maybe I should back this explanation up," Peter told them. "The only thing Xavier cares about is getting the amulet. And currently, his best way to acquire it is to mount a full-scale attack sometime in the summer. We are going to present him with a much more appealing option."

"Do explain," Mr. Winchester said from his rocking chair. "I like the sound of this."

"The note which Sapphire will take— or maybe I should say *get intercepted while taking*—to the lead weather gods, will include three things. Two of those will be written loud and clear, and the third will be hidden within the words. One: it will inform the lead weather gods about how we are planning to hide the amulet. Well, we won't really be hiding it that way, we just want Xavier to think so. Two: it will tell them the specific locations of where we want them to send help."

"And three?" Mr. Winchester asked. "The hidden message?"

"That," Peter smiled, "will tell Torin where to *really* send help. I'm banking on the fact that when Xavier intercepts the note, he'll see his opening. Instead of waiting weeks or months to launch an invasion, he'll lead a small group over immediately. But he'll think that we don't know he has discovered our plan."

"This is getting a little confusing," Demetrius admitted.

"Sorry," Peter apologized again. "Since Xavier will think he has the upper hand, he'll pretty much forget his plan to organize a big attack. He'll just rapidly grab a few of his best and bravest, come to Earth, and attempt to retrieve the amulet while we are still in the process of hiding it. But, we aren't hiding it, we are simply setting traps. And with those traps, we will catch Xavier and whoever else he brings along."

Mr. Winchester looked at Demetrius and smiled. "You owe me a dollar," he said to his friend. "I told you Peter's plan would involve some sort of smokescreen."

CHAPTER 6

Peter was pedaling like crazy to get home as quickly as possible. The first thing he needed to do was draft this tricky message, and that was going to require a considerable amount of time. Plus, he had at least an hour of history homework to complete (which he should have started a week ago, but had procrastinated about until the last minute...)

Peter leaned hard to his left to make the final turn on to Beaverbrook Street. (Wow, he could cook when riding Bradley's bike!)

* * *

2:51

With slightly over three hours until dinner, Peter set himself the goal of completing both the note and his homework before the clock struck six. (Shooting too high?)

"We both know you have been relegated to the second tier," he said to his pile of history stuff while tossing it on the bed to free up more space on his desk. "There won't be a world left to teach history to if we can't pull off this plan."

* * *

Peter's brain was capable of working at near-computer speeds when it came to mathematics, but creating this "note hidden within a note" was turning out to be extremely challenging.

"I wish Nik were here," he said to himself. "She's a genius when it comes to words."

That comment instantly brought Peter's train of thought to a halt. (He had been so busy contemplating their course of action to fool Xavier that he had completely forgotten about the yet-to-be-verified fact that his girlfriend went out with another guy last night!)

All of this was a little too much for poor Peter. He closed his eyes and tried to recall what his psychologist had advised him to do when he felt overwhelmed by circumstances that were out of his control.

"Remember, Peter," he said to himself in a very deep voice—trying to mimic the good doctor—"It's the way you are reacting to things that makes them bigger than they are. You can't change the facts, but you can, and must, choose how you react."

Peter shook his head. (Easier said than done, doc!)

* * *

He woke up from his unplanned afternoon nap at four forty-five. (Now he had one more thing to worry about: The amount of time he had just wasted!)

A common occurrence for people with obsessive-compulsive disorder was that a single worry could be (and often was) completely put aside when another one took its place at the top of the worry pile. Right now, all Peter could think about was his girlfriend's whereabouts last night between nine and ten.

"Remember Doctor Stanley's suggestion," Peter encouraged himself. "When you have a clear avenue to resolve a worry, you take it, without pausing or even thinking."

* * *

Twenty minutes later, Peter was still stalling on his bed, with the cordless phone lying beside him. He had had no issues about getting the phone or deciding to call Nicola, but he didn't want to dial until he knew exactly what he was going to say.

Peter was, either knowingly or unknowingly, torturing himself. He was trying to prepare not only how he was going to ask Nicola about last night, but also what he would say next depending on how she replied. (This was as hard as calculating chess moves against the computer!)

* * *

"Hey, what's up?" Nicola said right after her mom passed her the phone.

"Hey," Peter replied. (He hadn't thought about what to say if she asked that...) "How's it going?"

"Not bad," she replied. "Other than the fact that math is the most confusing subject on the face of the Earth."

"How was work last night?" Peter asked as casually as he could.

"Alright," she answered. "But I had two big groups of high school kids in my section, and they tipped me next to nothing."

"That sucks," Peter commented. "Any groups come in after eight? And make you have to work late like last week?" (That was the best way Peter had come up with to ask her about yesterday...)

"Thankfully, no," she replied right away. "I got off exactly at nine."

Silence... (She wasn't going to say any more...)

"Cool," Peter answered, chickening out about asking her for more details. "Anyway, I just wanted to see if you managed to get your history report done."

"Uh, Pete," she said back. "You must be tired or something. I finished it on Wednesday, and I even showed it to you after I finished."

Peter's armpits started sweating: That *cold, nervous* kind of sweat.

"That's right, you did," he said nervously, giggling a little. "Now I remember."

"Look, Pete," she said back. "Sorry to cut you off, but I really have to get back to studying. If I don't get at least a seventy on tomorrow's test, I'll end up with a *C* in math."

"Sorry," Peter said anxiously.

"See you tomorrow, bye," his girlfriend said while hanging up the phone. (She sure was in a hurry to finish that conversation...)

Peter's attempt to "squash his worry" had just done the exact opposite.

CHAPTER 7

Nicola was waiting just outside the door of their math classroom after the Monday morning test.

"I think I aced it!" she excitedly told Peter while hugging him. "Well, I doubt I got a hundred, but I'm sure I got at least eighty."

(Nicola was acting completely normal! Peter had spent all night worrying about nothing!)

"That's awesome," he said back, relieved to see that all was still fine with him and Nicola.

"And I owe a lot of that to you," she said, giving him a little peck on the cheek. "Your tutoring is the only reason I did so well."

"Don't sell yourself short," he told Nicola. "You worked hard. Give yourself most of the credit, not me."

Peter then spotted Neil heading out the door.

"Hey," he said to Neil. "How did you—"

"I failed," Neil said angrily without even

breaking stride. "I should have asked you to help me instead of Claire."

Peter didn't have a chance to ask Neil anything else, as his friend just kept right on walking.

Claire walked out next, but made no effort to catch up with Neil.

"What's up with your boyfriend?" Peter asked her. "Did he bomb the test that bad?"

"He did way worse than just bomb it," Claire answered. "And please don't call him my boyfriend anymore. As of yesterday afternoon, he officially became my *ex.*"

"Claire, meeting, now," a concerned Nicola said right away, taking Claire by the arm and walking away from Peter. She needed to find out exactly what was going on with Neil.

Peter shrugged his shoulders and started walking toward his next class. Halfway there, he decided to stop and use the washroom.

Just as he was about to enter the men's lavatory, Neil exited and slammed the door hard behind him. Peter had never seen Neil look this agitated before. (Neil was usually an extremely calm and collected kid, so this behavior was completely out of character.)

* * *

Peter ended up eating his lunch alone in front of his locker that day. Nicola had told him she was going to eat with Claire, and Neil must have felt like avoiding everyone.

Usually, Peter didn't entirely mind eating on his own. He wasn't exactly a "super social" person, and he was content to immerse himself in his thoughts. But today, he found himself having some difficulty pushing back his intrusive thoughts. Even though Nicola was acting normal, he still couldn't get Bradley's comment out of his mind... (Was Nicola only consoling Claire? Or was she also using this opportunity to tell Claire about how she secretly went on a date with another guy behind his back?)

CHAPTER 8

By the time Thursday rolled around, Nicola had filled Peter in on the status of Neil and Claire's relationship.

Because Neil always struggled with math, Claire had kindly offered to tutor him before the test. (For free, of course!)

But Neil didn't take their tutoring sessions seriously at all. He treated those afternoons together more like "dates." Claire had gotten testy with Neil on Sunday afternoon, and told him if he didn't start paying attention and acting his age, that he could learn math on his own.

For some reason, that comment rubbed Neil the wrong way. He told Claire (in a very rude tone) that he didn't need a second mother.

This escalated to the point where Claire picked up her books and stormed off. She was expecting Neil to follow her outside and apologize, but when he didn't, she turned around, walked right up to him, and dumped him.

But to be fair, Peter hadn't heard Neil's side of the story yet, as Neil still wasn't talking to anyone. He had tried phoning his friend a couple times, but during both attempts, Neil's mom had said her son couldn't come to the phone.

* * *

"Pete," Claire said to him at the start of lunch break on Friday. "Sorry for being so selfish this week."

"No problem," Peter replied.

"You mind if I eat lunch with you and Nik again today?" she asked them.

"Of course not," Nicola said right away, encouraging Claire to sit down beside them on the floor.

Peter felt quite uncomfortable, to say the least. He knew the whole story, but since Nicola was not supposed to have told him, he had to act like he didn't know…

* * *

"You guys busy tomorrow morning?" Peter asked the two girls a few minutes before the bell was set to ring. "We need to go to Mr. Winchester's." Peter paused and lowered his voice. "It's about X and Z."

Nicola and Claire both knew that speaking about weather gods in front of others was a big no-no, so they both responded with a thumbs up.

"But don't you dare invite Neil," Claire instructed Peter. "Okay?"

"Uh... okay," Peter replied. (He couldn't have answered in any other way, right?)

CHAPTER 9

When Peter told Bradley that they were heading to Mr. Winchester's house on Saturday, his older brother asked if his attendance was "compulsory" or not. Bradley wasn't trying to be sarcastic: It was just that he really wanted to go to his Saturday track and field practice. (A big competition was coming up soon, and Bradley was focused on performing well.)

And since Peter had to keep his promise to Claire, he didn't invite Neil. (Neil had technically been avoiding all of them, so it wasn't like Peter went out of his way to not bring up what they were doing.)

* * *

Peter, Nicola, and Claire met up shortly after eight on Saturday to start riding out to Mr. Winchester's place. Claire, thankfully, seemed a lot more chipper than yesterday. (Perhaps she was just happy to have something to distract herself from being angry at Neil?)

"Anything we need to know before we get there?" Nicola asked Peter, who was currently riding a few meters ahead.

"There's a lot to explain," Peter replied. "Probably easiest to wait till we are all there."

"You're the boss," Claire joked. "But at least tell us if it's good news or bad news."

"I don't think it falls into either of those categories," Peter replied, honestly not knowing if what they were going to discuss could be considered *completely positive* or *completely negative.* "It's more like, uh..."

"Like we gotta do something?" Claire asked him.

"That would be an oversimplification," Peter said back. "But yeah, I suppose that kind of sums it up."

CHAPTER 10

Because it was such a beautiful spring morning in Clearville, Mr. Winchester, Zoltan, and his parents were all sipping their coffees on the front porch when Peter and his friends arrived.

"Can I get you three a coffee?" Mr. Winchester asked as they walked up the front steps.

"I'd love one," Nicola answered. "But I'll go in and pour them. You can stay out here and relax."

"Sure, I'll have a cup too, Nik," Claire told her friend. "Milk, no sugar."

"Gotcha," Nicola replied. "Pete?"

"Maybe later," he answered. (But when Peter said *later,* he was probably referring to when he reached his twentieth birthday!)

* * *

There was no urgency to jump into the brainstorming session immediately, so they spent the first little while sitting in the sunshine and chatting.

"And before we hear this marvelous and

mysterious plan Peter has drawn up for defeating Xavier," Mr. Winchester said when everyone's coffee cups were empty, "we have a little surprise for you."

"A surprise?" Peter asked. "But wait, it isn't any of our birthdays or anything like that."

"I don't know how many more of your birthdays I'll be around for," Mr. Winchester laughed. "I'm not getting any younger."

"He's right," Sapphire added. "And old folks like us just love doing things for kids we care about."

"And technically," Demetrius said next. "We aren't really *giving* you anything. It's more like we are challenging you to do something."

"You made a puzzle for us?" Peter asked excitedly.

"Two, in fact," Zoltan smiled. "My parents came up with one, and Mr. Winchester with the other."

"Cool," Claire said. "Where are they?"

Sapphire walked up and passed Claire an envelope. "Go around back," she told them. "Everything is set up in the backyard."

Peter was on his way before he'd even had a chance to say, "Thanks!"

CHAPTER 11

Beside the barbeque, there is a bucket of marbles. And at the far end of the yard, there is an empty bucket.

Task: You...

"What does it say next?" Nicola asked Peter, who had suddenly stopped reading.

"That's it," Peter replied. "It's like—"

"My apologies," Mr. Winchester said as he rounded the corner to the backyard. "I forgot to mention that to Sapphire: I figured it would be easier to tell you the rules instead of writing everything down."

"We're all ears," Claire said happily.

"The buckets themselves cannot be moved or tipped over," Mr. Winchester began. "The task here is to get all the marbles from this bucket into the other one. And you may make multiple trips back and forth to do this. But there are some crucial rules that must be followed: All three of you must walk together when you move from one bucket to the other. Every time you move, all three of you must be carrying the exact same number of marbles. So let's say Peter picks up 25: Then Claire and Nicola must also take 25 each. And, of course, you are only allowed to carry the marbles in your hands."

"How many are there in total?" Peter asked.

"Telling you that," Mr. Winchester smiled, "would only spoil part of the fun."

"Do we have a time limit?" Nicola asked.

"Not for this challenge," Demetrius replied. "Alright, good luck!"

"Oops," Mr. Winchester said, giggling at his forgetfulness. "There was one thing I forgot to mention: When you are putting the marbles in the far bucket, you must drop them in."

* * *

The bucket contained A LOT of marbles. There was no way to even venture a guess at how many, but if someone told them to ballpark it, Peter would have said *a couple hundred.*

"Since we are not allowed to tip the bucket," Peter began. "Maybe the easiest way to do this is to take an amount we can easily count and carry. How about... say... 20 each? So that means 60 between the three of us each time."

"Sure," Nicola agreed. "Plus that's an amount we can surely remember."

"And few enough that we won't drop any," Claire added.

Claire squatted down beside the bucket and started taking out two at a time with her right hand and putting them into her left hand. "Let's do 15 instead of 20, she suggested. "These marbles are bigger than I thought."

"Gotcha," Nicola agreed as she started to count her 15.

When all three were ready, they walked to the far pail, dropped their marbles in it, and returned to the first bucket again.

"This is gonna take a while," Peter remarked.

"Think of it as exercise, Peter," Mr. Winchester joked. (And that got all the adults laughing!)

* * *

After their sixth trip, the bucket by the barbeque was finally close to being empty.

"I'll count out exactly how many are remaining," Claire told her team. "Then we just split that number by three."

* * *

"21, 22, 23," she said. "23 in total."

"23?" Peter asked her back. "You sure?"

"I think so," she replied. "But let me drop them back in one by one to double-check."

Sure enough, there were 23 marbles.

"Well, 23 is not divisible by 3," Peter mentioned, pointing out the obvious.

"I guess we must have made a counting error

in one of our first six trips," Claire said.

Getting the marbles back to the original bucket was no fun, since the rules for this challenge basically made the only way to transport them back the same as how they had just taken them there: Moving back and forth as a team, always carrying the same number of marbles each.

* * *

"Should we take 10 each instead of 15 this time?" Claire suggested before beginning their second attempt. "That would make it less likely for us to make a mistake."

"Sure, makes sense," Peter said.

The next fifteen minutes were painstakingly boring, and little was said other than *numbers.* But they didn't want to botch up their counting again, so they double-checked that each one of them had exactly 10 each time before they started walking.

* * *

"How many trips have we made?" Nicola asked. "I've completely lost count."

"Nine," Peter answered instantly.

"Looks like there are less than 30 left in the pail," Claire smiled. "Here, put your hands out, I'll put one at a time, in each person's palm, until they are all gone."

* * *

"6, 6, 6, 7, 7, 7," she said as the bucket neared

emptiness. "8, 8…" She paused… "No, not again!"

"There's no way we screwed up our counting this time," Nicola complained. "We were extra, extra careful."

"How do we split 23 marbles three ways?" Claire asked. "Are we supposed to smash one in half?"

"None of the marbles need to be harmed in any way," Zoltan said sarcastically from his comfortable lawn chair.

HI READER! (^_^)
ANY IDEA WHAT THEY SHOULD DO? CAN'T SPLIT 23 MARBLES 3 WAYS!

CHAPTER 12

"I hope this doesn't sound condescending," Nicola said timidly, "but nothing we've done so far has involved any, uh... thinking."

Peter smiled. "You're right," he said. "We were just absent-mindedly transferring marbles."

Mr. Winchester had been daydreaming, but came back to the present when he heard that comment. "I was wondering how long it would take you to turn your brains on," he joked.

Peter walked over to the patio table and picked up the three remaining glasses of lemonade that Zoltan had brought out a little earlier. He passed one to Nicola and one to Claire. Then the three sat cross-legged on the lush grass.

"At least today's puzzle is just for fun," Peter mentioned to the girls. "Sure is much less stressful when the fate of the world isn't hanging on a thread."

"No kidding," Claire commented. "So Pete, uh... any ideas?"

"Let's finish our lemonade first," Peter replied. "Then we can regroup and refocus."

* * *

"We either need a way to get one extra marble," Peter said right after his last gulp of juice, "or a way to make two disappear."

"Then we would have either 21 or 24, right?" Claire added. "Which we could split 3 ways."

"Can't we just carry one back?" Nicola suggested. "He never said we couldn't do that."

"But remember," Peter said. "The three of us always have to move together, and always carry the same number of marbles."

"Oh," Nicola nodded. "If we want to bring any marbles back, the minimum would be 1 marble each, so a total of 3 then, right?"

"Which wouldn't solve our problem," Claire added.

"More lemonade anyone?" Demetrius asked loudly. "I'm going inside to make a second pitcher."

"Sure," Peter replied right away. "But no ice this time, please."

"No ice?" Demetrius asked.

"The cold bothers one of my bicuspids," Peter explained.

"Your what?" Demetrius inquired (with a very confused expression on his face.)

"Demetrius," Nicola said in an effort to help. "Claire and I are both good with no ice as well."

Then she leaned over and whispered to Peter and Claire, "No need to confuse the poor old guy, right?"

* * *

Claire, who had been stretching her legs while trying to come up with an idea of what to do next, stopped suddenly... and then looked over at her friends.

"Got something?" Peter asked her.

"I certainly do," she replied, smiling.

"Awesome!" Nicola cheered. "That didn't take long."

"Guys, put your hands out," Claire said excitedly.

She gave 7 marbles to Nicola, 7 to Peter, and took 7 for herself.

"Okay, let's go and dump these in the other bucket," she instructed them.

Claire looked quite satisfied to be the one that had determined the solution, so she was walking proudly (and so fast that Peter and Nicola had to jog to keep up!)

They dropped all 21 marbles in the bucket.

"When carrying the marbles from one bucket to the other," she began, "we have to carry the same number each time, right?"

Both Peter and Nicola wanted to say they already knew that, but figured Claire was about to unveil what they had both missed.

Claire reached into the full bucket, picked up

one marble, got into a baseball pitching stance, and smirked.

"Claire," Nicola said shyly. "Didn't Mr. Winchester say we have to drop them in the bucket?"

"He only said we had to drop them in THIS bucket," Claire told her. "But throwing one BACK doesn't break any rules."

Peter grinned. Brilliant!

"But how are you going to get it to land in the first bucket?" Nicola asked. "You'd have to have a perfect throw."

"I don't have to get it *in* the bucket," Claire answered. "Just somewhere close."

Claire chucked the marble. It bounced a couple times in the grass and came to a stop about a meter to the right of the bucket.

"Nice arm," Peter commended her.

The three energetic and excited teenagers raced back. Peter and Nicola picked up one marble each (from the bucket) which left it empty, and Claire picked up the one she had just thrown back.

As they walked toward the far bucket triumphantly, Mr. Winchester started clapping. "Well done!" he exclaimed. "Well done, indeed!"

Claire was so happy that she decided to strut the final few meters. As soon as they dropped the final 3 marbles in, there were big high-fives all around.

"And before you walk back," Mr. Winchester yelled to them. "Look on the back of that tree trunk: Your second riddle is there."

Peter peered around the thick tree and saw where the envelope had been tacked to it.

"Cool," he said. "Is this, like, part two of what we just finished?"

"Nope," Demetrius answered. "This is your... homework. Just stick it in your pocket and give it a go sometime later."

"Homework?" Nicola asked, laughing.

(Homework was usually tedious, but this was the kind Peter would never complain about!)

"And now we had better get down to business," Demetrius suggested. "We have loads to get through today."

Peter had been enjoying himself so thoroughly that he had almost forgotten why they were here in the first place!

CHAPTER 13

"It's unfortunate that Neil and Bradley were unable to join us today," Mr. Winchester innocently said as everyone got comfortable in the living room.

Hearing Neil's name made Peter immediately feel uneasy. He forced himself to keep looking straight ahead, so he wouldn't have to make eye-contact with Claire.

And Claire, of course, was seething because the mention of her selfish ex-boyfriend had just spoiled her elated mood.

Nicola sensed all this tension and decided to help everyone by deflecting the issue. "Yeah, Brad and Neil are both busy," she said quickly. "Anyway, Pete tells me we are going to be setting a trap for Xavier. Is that even possible?"

"If anyone can come up with a plan that will work," Demetrius commented, "it's our Peter."

Peter blushed. (Well, just a little...)

"Have you had any luck writing the note that I

will be delivering?" Sapphire asked Peter.

He reached in his backpack and pulled it out.

"This is just the first draft," he told everyone. "I wanted to get your feedback. And then once I've made changes, we'll get Mr. Winchester to hand-write the final version. We need to make sure they think the message came from him."

Everyone gathered around Peter.

Dear Lead Weather Gods,

I'm sending this message to you, via the trusted hands of Sapphire, as I fear Xavier's army may come here soon and attempt to steal the amulet. Unfortunately, I don't think we can hold them off on our own. We need help, and you are our second-to-last option. Everything I've written here, from the next line on, will explain what we are planning, and exactly what we need you to do:

We will be hiding the amulet.

And we desperately need help protecting it.

I am including 3 sets of coordinates on this page.

Please send whoever you can to these spots, to help us fight.

And send them before it's too late.

With enough on our side, we can hold Xavier off.

But without help, our chances are slim.

And the consequences of losing are huge.

Loyally yours,

Leonardo

52°44'2"N   7°14'48"W
31°35'49"N   34°54'2"E
29°3'42"N   119°11'3"E

"Are those actual locations of real places here on Earth?" Demetrius asked. "Or just spots in the middle of nowhere?"

"Oh, those are more than just random coordinates," Peter explained. "They all have some type of caves or tunnels or ancient ruins. They'll be ideal places for us to set the traps."

"Fantastic!" Zoltan exclaimed. "But as much as

I hate to admit this, I am completely unable to find that hidden message for Torin."

"Same here," Demetrius said. "You sure he won't miss it?"

Mr. Winchester was smiling. "Torin will definitely spot the message," he told everyone, obviously having deciphered it already. "It might take him a minute or two, but he'll notice it."

"Let me read that note again," Demetrius said, gesturing for Peter to pass him the paper. "I'm certainly not going to let Leonardo one-up me."

Everyone laughed. Once a puzzler, always a puzzler!

HI READER! (^_^)
CAN YOU FIGURE OUT THE SECRET MESSAGE FOR TORIN?

CHAPTER 14

Peter then explained to everyone that what they needed to accomplish first was to construct some special boxes: just like the one they had used to trap Xavier when they had staged that fake ceremony for him.

He showed them the list of the materials that were required to build each one, plus a sketch (with accurate dimensions, of course!) of the original trap they had previously used.

"How many do you want to build?" Demetrius asked Peter.

"The more the merrier," he replied. "At least six or seven... Well, ten or twelve would be ideal."

Mr. Winchester scanned the list. "We can probably purchase everything at the local hardware store," he said. "But I doubt they'll have enough stock to build more than a few."

"We could head to Stoneburg," Peter suggested. "There's a massive home and garden center there."

"But how are we going to transport everything back here so we can build them?" Claire asked. "Or, well, how are we even going to get to Stoneburg in the first place? None of us has a car."

"Brad can drive us tomorrow morning," Peter said confidently. "And we wouldn't have to haul the stuff back. That store has a delivery service. It's not free, but—"

"The last thing anyone needs to concern themselves with is the cost," Mr. Winchester said. "We have plenty of money."

Nicola was in the room, but seemed somewhat removed from the conversation. Not only that, but she had been looking down at her watch pretty frequently. "Sorry to be rude," she said quite unexpectedly, "but I start work earlier than usual today. I gotta run."

"Of course, Nicola," Zoltan said politely. "Not to worry, Peter can fill you in on the rest later."

"But it's only ten forty-five," Peter said to his girlfriend. "What time do you start?"

"I don't have a specific start time today," she replied awkwardly. "Travis asked me to come in early if I could. He's short-staffed or something."

"Oh," Peter replied. (Travis??)

The story Bradley had told him—the one he wanted to vacate from his memory—jumped front and center again.

"Pete," she said while putting on her shoes.

"Just phone my mom tonight and tell her what time you guys will pick me up tomorrow."

"Okay," Peter replied. (Did he mask the suspicion and worry in his voice?)

* * *

Later that day, after what turned into a very long and draining afternoon, Peter and Claire began riding back home. Although they knew each other fairly well, both felt a little weird right now. (Well, Claire felt a little weird. It was Peter who was uncomfortable...)

This was the first time for them to ever be alone together. And not only that, but Peter was super stressed out: He currently had way too many thoughts racing through his head about what this Travis guy was up to.

"Who's Travis?" Claire asked. (That was the last question Peter was expecting! Had she just read Peter's mind?)

"Dunno," he answered, trying to sound like he didn't care.

"Wait a second," she said after that. "I know exactly who Travis is! Travis Penner! He's in Grade 12. He's this tall and really cute guy. Don't you know who I'm talking about?"

"No clue," Peter told her. (He was being honest. He didn't know any of the Grade 12s.)

"Look, I hope this doesn't make you worry even more," she said next. "But Travis would be on any girl's *top three hottest guys in the school* list."

"Do girls actually write lists like that?" Peter asked.

"Of course not," she laughed. "I meant that figuratively."

"Oh," he said, a little stuck for words.

"Let me investigate things a little," she told Peter. "I'll make some calls when I get home. I've got a friend whose sister is friends with a friend of Travis."

"Um…" Peter mumbled, trying to figure out exactly how that connection worked. "Okay, thanks." He paused a bit. "But… uh… what are you gonna ask?"

"Not sure," she replied. "But I'll think of an inconspicuous way to find out. Don't worry, no one will ever know I'm your private detective." She giggled a little. "Plus, it'll distract me from thinking about Neil."

(Oops, Peter had kind of forgotten about that…)

"Has he said ANYTHING to you about me?" she asked.

"He's been completely avoiding me," Peter told her. "Do you want me to call him?"

"Absolutely not!" Claire replied sharply. "He deserves to feel alienated right now."

"Okay," Peter said. (Now he was feeling just as uncomfortable as before this conversation began…)

CHAPTER 15

After saying goodbye to Claire, Peter began pondering if he should or shouldn't intervene in the whole Neil-Claire saga before heading home. He liked them both, and truly wanted to see them bury the hatchet and make up.

"Regretting something you didn't do," Peter told himself, "is ten times worse than regretting something you did but wish you hadn't."

Mind made up, he took a short detour to Neil's house. He knew Neil would be home, as he never worked on Saturdays anymore. (Neil's mom was only permitting him to work Sundays until his grades improved.)

* * *

"Oh, Peter," Neil's mom said happily as she opened the front door. "Neil's up in his room."

"Hi Mrs. Bannister," Peter replied politely. Then he quickly remembered Neil's mom had changed her last name after the divorce. "Sorry, I mean Mrs. Wright. I apologize for dropping by without calling first." Then he *fibbed* a little. "There's a school project due this week that Neil and I are working on together."

"Lucky Neil!" she said. "Odds are very good he'll get an *A* then."

Peter blushed. "Neil always does his fair share," he lied.

"Neil! Peter's here!" she shouted upstairs.

A few seconds later, Neil came to the top of the stairs. His hair was scruffy and he was still wearing his pajamas. "What do you want?" he asked coldly.

"You watch your attitude," his mom scolded him. "You should be grateful that Peter puts up with you."

"Sorry, Mom," Neil said, realizing fully well that he was in the wrong. Neil and his mom had always had a close bond, which had become even stronger the day his dad had left their family for a younger woman years back. "Come on up," he said to Peter while turning to go back into his room.

* * *

Neil was standing in his room with his arms crossed when Peter entered. "Close the door," he ordered Peter in an angry tone.

Peter shut the door, but before he had a chance to say anything, Neil was in his face.

"I know exactly why you're here," he told Peter. "You're trying to get Claire and me back together.

Well, you're wasting your time. And your breath. It's done, I'm moving on."

Peter couldn't tell if Neil was being truthful or not. Of course, he did want the formerly happy couple to smooth things over, but today was not going to be the day for that.

Peter needed to think quickly. (How could he "arrange" for Neil and Claire to be in the same place?) He grabbed Neil's desk chair, spun it around, and sat down.

"The reason I came over has nothing to do with Claire," he said.

"Oh, come on," Neil barked back. "Why else would you just show up out of nowhere?"

Peter lowered his voice a little. "Xavier and some of his evil crew are coming to Earth sometime soon," he whispered. "We need your help."

Neil froze. And the expression on his face changed immediately.

"Xavier's coming? When?" he asked.

"Have a seat," Peter told his friend. "I'll explain everything from the beginning."

* * *

Peter's very detailed account of their plan to trap Xavier and his evil colleagues was sufficient to get Neil up to speed.

"We need your help," he said at the end. "We HAVE TO make this plan work."

"But Claire's helping too, right?" Neil inquired.

"Yes, of course she is," Peter answered. "Look, I don't care if you guys speak to each other or not. I'm thinking about the bigger picture here: If we fail, Xavier gets the amulet. If Xavier gets the amulet, we, and tons of other people, get tortured or possibly even killed."

"Suppose I don't have a choice then, do I?" Neil asked.

"You do have a choice," Peter said with conviction in his voice. "But if you choose not to help just because your silly pride won't allow you to be in the same place as your ex-girlfriend, and then I fail, are you prepared to live with the consequences?"

"But didn't you just say we'd all probably die if you failed?" Neil asked. (Neil was missing the point...)

"I'll take that comment as a 'Yes, I'll help,'" Peter smiled.

CHAPTER 16

The trip to Stoneburg Home Center on Sunday morning was an overwhelming success. The huge store had everything they needed, and tons of it.

To help save them all the time and energy required to cut everything to size, Mr. Winchester inquired as to how much it would cost for the store to do that for them. After calculating the cutting charge and explaining that they would need a few days to do it, Mr. Winchester made an offer: He said he'd pay an extra two hundred and fifty dollars if they cut everything this morning, and delivered it this afternoon.

The store manager immediately pushed their order to the front of the line.

* * *

During the ride back, Peter prepared to make his announcement to Claire about Neil. He had decided to wait until this specific moment because then she would be in a position to tell Bradley to drop her off at home if she was too angry.

"Claire," he said nervously. "You're gonna hate me when I tell you this, but Neil's coming over to Mr. Winchester's this afternoon."

"You better be joking," she said, clearly unimpressed. "I specifically told you to stay out of this."

"I'm sorry," he apologized. "Look, I didn't say anything about *you* to him. All I told Neil was that we need him on our team, because we do. And, well, he agreed."

"I know you're trying to get us to make up," she blurted out at Peter.

"Claire, please," Peter pleaded again. "We need Neil and we need you. You don't have to talk to him. You don't even have to look at him."

Claire crossed her arms and stared out the window. (All things considered, this was a pretty good outcome. At least she didn't announce she was quitting the team!)

And the rest of the drive back was horribly uncomfortable and silent.

CHAPTER 17

Zoltan and his parents had prepared an exorbitant feast for lunch. It looked like the kind of meal that would be served to visiting kings and queens.

"How many people did you guys think were coming?" Bradley jokingly asked. "There's enough food here to feed my whole track team at college. Twice."

"I suppose we might have gone a little overboard," Demetrius admitted. "We were having way too much fun cooking with all these ingredients we'd never seen or heard of before."

Bradley went to help himself to one of the crackers with smoked salmon and cream cheese on it, but Sapphire lightly slapped the back of his hand before he touched the scrumptious-looking appetizer.

"We will not be eating until the clock strikes twelve," she told him. "And it's currently only a quarter past eleven."

"Come on, just one?" Bradley begged, laughing. "My stomach is rumbling as loud as a truck."

Sapphire smirked. "Okay, but only one," she told Bradley. "You just said so yourself."

"Coffee's ready!" Demetrius announced from the kitchen. "Get it while it's hot!"

It was another beautiful day, so they took their coffees—even Peter decided to try one today—to the patio out back. The conversation was like a pinball machine: It kept bouncing around from topic to topic, with no one knowing what was going to be brought up next.

* * *

At 11:58, Sapphire told everyone they could come inside for lunch. She and Demetrius had set up the dining room table as a buffet. They thought it would be perfect for everyone to fill up their plates and take them back outside to eat. Bradley moved so fast for the food that it was almost like he had teleported himself there. Plus, he stacked so much on his plate that it formed a mountain.

No more than five minutes later, they were all back outside, eating and chatting away. Everyone was commenting on how delicious the meal was when the doorbell rang.

"Looks like that two hundred and fifty bucks inspired them to cut like crazy," Bradley commented. "They must have started on it the second we left the store."

"Hold on," Zoltan said, standing up. "Didn't you say they would drop it off this afternoon? There's no way they could have cut everything that fast."

"Are you expecting any other deliveries?" Claire asked Mr. Winchester.

"No, not that I can recall," he replied.

The doorbell rang again.

"I don't like this," Zoltan said. "Something seems wrong."

"So what should we do?" Peter asked quietly.

"We all hide in the kitchen," Zoltan whispered. "Leonardo will open the door a crack, but keep the chain on."

"You think it's one of Xavier's guys, don't you?" Nicola asked.

"We have to be as careful as possible," Demetrius replied. "Come on, let's get ready. If someone doesn't answer the door soon, whoever it is may come around back."

Zoltan had the amulet in his pocket and was hiding inside the front door, out of sight. If it was an evil weather god, he would be able to react instantaneously.

"Coming!" Mr. Winchester said loudly while walking to the door. "I was just using the washroom!"

He double-checked the chain was in place, unlocked the deadbolt, and then twisted the handle.

CHAPTER 18

"Neil?" Mr. Winchester said, flabbergasted to see who was standing on his front porch. Then he turned around and loudly announced, "Everyone! It's just Neil!"

He closed the door so he could undo the chain, and then quickly opened it back up to welcome in his guest. Everyone who had been hiding in the kitchen—with the exception of Claire—came out to say hi.

"I was just about to hop back on my bike and head home," he told them. "But since Brad's car was out front, I figured you had to be here."

"My sincerest apologies," Mr. Winchester said while shaking Neil's hand. "We are all a little on edge."

"I thought you worked until two today?" Peter asked.

"Oh," Neil replied. "I asked my boss if I could leave early: I told him I needed to do an important assignment."

"You lied to your boss?" Nicola questioned him.

"No," Neil answered, smiling. "I never said it was a *school* assignment. Plus, I would consider helping save the Earth from an apocalypse to be quite important."

Everyone laughed.

"Help yourself to some lunch," Sapphire said welcomingly. "And join us out back."

"Don't mind if I do," Neil said, going to grab a plate to fill up with the assortment of extravagant foods.

But to get to the dining room, he needed to walk through the kitchen, which meant walking past Claire. Their eyes met for a brief instant, but not a single word was uttered.

Neil piled up an almost-Bradley-sized pile of food on his plate and walked out the back sliding doors to join everyone.

"Since Neil's here now," Peter suggested. "Why don't I explain the parts of the plan I haven't talked about yet?"

"No time better than the present," Mr. Winchester agreed, very eager to hear this for himself.

"Those three locations I indicated in the letter," Peter began, "are the spots where we are going to set up some challenges."

"Challenges?" Bradley asked. "But I thought we were trying to trap them."

"We are," Peter answered. "But we need a way

to get them to... well... unknowingly walk into the boxes we are building."

"Let me make sure I am following you," Demetrius commented. "You want us to set up challenges at these three locations. Whoever comes, of course, will expect that they can reach the amulet by completing the challenge."

"Exactly," Peter replied. "We also need to be at all three places to monitor what they are doing. So we can, um... react, if necessary."

"Who do you mean by *we?*" Zoltan asked. "And you'll need to clarify the meaning of *react.*"

"Hold on a sec," Peter said, putting his plate on the table and reaching into his backpack. "I need to check my notes."

A few seconds later, he continued, "I've split us up into three teams: Mr. Winchester and I will go to location one, Nik and Neil will go to number two, and Claire and Brad to three. I'm also hoping to assign a couple weather gods to each spot as well, but I can't sort that out until we see how many Torin can round up."

"But how are we going to get to these three places?" Claire asked. (That was the first time she had spoken since Neil's arrival!) "They are all on opposite sides of the globe."

Zoltan smiled. "I've got us covered," he told the teenagers. "Thanks to this amulet, I can fly us at speeds that would leave the fastest rockets on this planet in our dust."

"Peter," Sapphire said next. "When do you think I should use Leonardo's ship to deliver the note to Torin?"

"The sooner, the better," he replied. "But first, we need to have all the boxes built and the challenges completely set up."

"Hey," Bradley said to everyone. "I know how we can get those boxes built lickety-split."

"How?" Peter asked his brother.

"I'll tell my track and field team that I have volunteered them to help construct something," he explained. "College students are always looking to volunteer for stuff, right? It looks good on their resume."

"But we can't risk them knowing about all this," Demetrius said, sounding concerned.

"I'll just say the boxes are part of the set for a magic show," Bradley told them. "They probably won't even care. Anyway, tomorrow morning after practice, I'll get as many people as I can to come here to build. We'll have them all done by dinner."

"And once they are done," Zoltan added, "I can start transporting them to the three locations."

"And when exactly will we set up the challenges?" Nicola asked.

"Well, we've got school all week," Peter answered, "so the soonest we can do it is this coming Saturday."

"Or," Zoltan suggested, "if you give us a detailed description of each challenge, we could do the set-up during the week."

"If these preparations go smoothly," Mr. Winchester said, thinking aloud, "then Sapphire should be able to depart on Saturday, or Sunday at the latest."

Peter felt his heart skip a beat. A week from today, they would be dangling the bait for Xavier. (He just hoped Torin could send enough weather gods to give them a fighting chance...)

CHAPTER 19

Bradley had managed to bring about eighty percent of his track team—twenty-six college students in total—to assist with the construction of the boxes. They were a very close-knit group, so they joked and laughed while working feverishly all Monday afternoon.

Mr. Winchester, Zoltan, and his parents were doing everything they could to keep the "workers" fully nourished and sufficiently hydrated. (And they were blown away by the amount of food these young adults could consume!)

"These kids eat like horses," Sapphire had said, "but they don't appear to have a single ounce of fat on their bodies."

By around four thirty, they had put the finishing touches on the twelfth and final box. Then they double-checked to ensure each one was completely sealed from outside light: a crucial point that couldn't be missed.

* * *

"Done and dusted," Bradley said to Peter—who was plugging away at homework at his desk—at a little past five in the afternoon.

"You guys built *all* of them?" Peter asked Bradley. "In half a day?"

"We don't mess around," Bradley replied.

"Brad, would you please take a shower? You smell awful!" his mom yelled from downstairs while pinching her nose. She had just come back from grocery shopping and was about to ask her sons to come and help carry in all the food. "Pete, I need a hand."

* * *

Peter dialed Mr. Winchester right after he had finished putting the supermarket haul away. (It wouldn't have taken so long if his mom wasn't such a perfectionist.) Not only did everything have to go in the correct spots, but the labels had to be facing forward, and the newest boxes and cans needed to be put at the back of each row.

"Your brother and his friends did an immaculate job," Mr. Winchester told Peter. "Zoltan will start delivering the boxes to those three destinations first thing tomorrow."

"Perfect," Peter replied. "Tell you what, why don't Nik and I drop by tomorrow after school? I managed to finish deciding on all the challenges, so I need to show you the list of supplies."

"Sure," his old friend replied. "But how did you find time to do so much in less than twenty-four hours? Weren't you at school all day today?"

Peter smiled smugly to himself. "I did it during class," he said. "And it was the first time in as long as I can remember that I enjoyed being at school."

Mr. Winchester laughed into the receiver. "But don't you go and let your grades slip," he said. "I don't want your angry mother hunting me down!"

CHAPTER 20

Peter was waiting for Nicola outside her drama classroom door after period two on Tuesday morning.

"Nik," he said casually. "I'm heading to Mr. Winchester's after school. Can you come?"

Instead of taking Peter's hand or putting her arm around his waist—which almost seemed to be second nature by now—she replied, "Sorry, I gotta work on my geography report after school." She kept walking past him without even slowing down. "Just call me when you get back."

It kind of made sense that she left Peter on his own during the ten-minute break, as their third-period classes were different (and on opposite sides of the school), but the little worrier inside Peter's brain couldn't dispel the fact that she was acting oddly. (Or was he just imagining things?)

* * *

Peter had brought the challenge supplies list

with him to school: that way he could go straight to Mr. Winchester's after the final bell rang. But he still had thirty minutes of math class left before he could start riding. He had finished the pages his class was working on over fifteen minutes ago, so he, literally, had nothing to do other than just wait.

Thankfully, Peter remembered he had something in his backpack that was sure to speed up the movement of the slowly ticking clock.

When his teacher was helping a student on the far side of the room, Peter reached in his backpack and removed the puzzle Mr. Winchester had made a few days ago. He unfolded it and quickly hid it under his textbook. He was planning on reading it in bits and pieces, all while constantly checking to make sure Mrs. Moorhouse wasn't coming his way.

Mrs. Waterton, a kind and caring mother and grandmother, loved baking for her family. She especially liked making cookies, as they were her grandchildren's favorite.

Early in the morning of her eldest granddaughter Emily's twelfth birthday, she baked a huge batch, knowing the smile it would bring to Emily's face. Emily came downstairs even before her parents had woken up, as the wonderful smell had drifted up to her room.

At her spot at the table, there was a plate with four freshly baked cookies on it.

After receiving a big birthday hug, she sat down and got ready to devour this special treat.

Just before Emily was about to grab a cookie, her grandmother said she had prepared a little birthday game.

She told her granddaughter that she had folded up a ten-dollar bill, and hidden it under one of the chocolate chip cookies. If Emily could guess which cookie it was under on her first try, she would not only get that ten dollars, but also an extra ten as well.

Emily pointed at one of the four cookies. Her grandmother lifted it, unveiling the folded bill!

Emily was now twenty dollars richer! What a birthday!

But how did she know which cookie it was under?

"Peter... PETER!" Mrs. Moorhouse said loudly. (The entire class was now looking at him...)

"Umm... yes?" he replied.

"You know you shouldn't be reading love letters during math class," she said while coming over and snatching the riddle from his hands.

Everyone burst out laughing.

But Peter was getting a little better at not letting things like this overly bother him, so he only blushed a bit, and didn't start sweating at all. (Plus, his photographic memory wouldn't forget what he had just read, so his mind was going to be happily busy during the remainder of this dreary mathematics lesson!)

CHAPTER 21

"I thought Nicola was coming over too?" Mr. Winchester asked after letting Peter in shortly past three o'clock.

"She wanted to come," he replied, "but she's behind on one of her reports. She had to go straight home after school." (Peter realized that not everything he had just said was completely true, but he wasn't in the mood to discuss his girlfriend issues right now...)

"I have some good news to report," Mr. Winchester told his young friend. "Zoltan has already dropped off five of the boxes, and is currently out delivering the sixth."

"But isn't that a lot of work?" Peter asked.

"Yes, he is doing too much," Sapphire commented. "But it's such a relief to see him committed to helping. He's so passionate about doing everything he can to help Earth."

"And you are the main reason for his change in attitude," Demetrius added.

"I'd say Mr. Winchester is the person who deserves all the credit," Peter admitted. "He worked his butt off for over twenty-five years trying to steer Zoltan in the right direction."

"Oh, Peter," Mr. Winchester laughed. "Too humble to accept your deserved recognition."

Peter's face was a tad bit red now. To try to mask this, he reached into his backpack and started filing through it for the list. "I know it's in here somewhere," he mumbled. When he finally found it—over two minutes later—he approached Mr. Winchester in the big rocking chair to hand it over.

But Mr. Winchester was already up, and was slowly making his way toward his bedroom.

"Just leave it with Demetrius," he said without looking back. "I'll take a look at it a little later."

Peter was unsure of how to react. (Was Mr. Winchester in a bad mood about something? Or maybe he was a little under the weather?)

Once he heard the bedroom door shut, Peter softly asked Demetrius and Sapphire, "Is he alright?"

"Let's talk outside," Sapphire replied right away.

They went out to the front porch, as the back patio was too close to Mr. Winchester's bedroom.

"He made us swear we would never tell you this," Sapphire began. "But Leonardo has been having chest pains and shortness of breath recently."

"Then he needs to go to a hospital right away," Peter said. "Or at least to a drop-in clinic."

"We have told him the exact same thing numerous times," Demetrius told Peter, "but Leonardo can be extremely stubborn. He promised us he would go as soon as Sapphire returns from Sevlar."

"But chest pains are considered a medical emergency," Peter said. "This isn't something that can wait."

"You are welcome to tell him that when he wakes up from his nap," Sapphire advised Peter. "But it won't do you any good. If you want him to go to a hospital, you'll have to drag him there kicking and screaming."

"Hold on," Peter said, opening the front door and heading back inside. "I think I have an idea."

He grabbed the cordless phone from the living room and brought it outside to ensure Mr. Winchester wouldn't overhear the call. He had already dialed his home number, and had the receiver up to his ear when he closed the door behind him.

"Yo," Bradley said when he picked up the phone. (He certainly wouldn't have said that if his parents were at home!)

"Brad, it's me," Peter said, speaking quickly. "I need you to come to Mr. Winchester's A.S.A.P."

"Uh... okay, what's up?" Bradley asked.

"I'll explain when you get here," he told his older brother. "We'll be waiting out front."

"Roger," Bradley said back. "See you in ten."

* * *

"Sounds like a good plan to me," Bradley told Peter after hearing about Mr. Winchester's current health issues and Peter's idea about how to get him to the hospital. "We pretend the five of us are going out to dinner, and you and I are treating everyone."

"And then instead of driving to a restaurant in Stoneburg, where we pretend to have made a reservation," Peter repeated to Bradley, "you drive straight to the hospital, pull up to emergency, and I'll run in and tell them we brought an elderly man with chest pains."

"And the ER staff will bolt out right away," Bradley nodded. "Sounds good. But Pete, he's gonna hate us for this."

"Probably," Peter replied. "But at least he'll be alive."

* * *

"What's the special occasion?" Mr. Winchester asked from the passenger seat as Bradley drove their entourage down the highway to Stoneburg.

"Who says we need a special occasion to take you guys out?" Peter said from the backseat. "Just imagine this is the entire human race's way of saying *Thank You.*"

"In that case," Mr. Winchester laughed, "I

suppose I don't feel guilty."

* * *

A few minutes later, when Bradley went through downtown Stoneburg without stopping, Mr. Winchester seemed to sense something was going on.

"Bradley," the old man inquired. "I believe you have just passed all the restaurants. Are you sure you know where you're headed?"

"Positive," Bradley replied, eyes looking straight ahead.

Peter, Demetrius, or Sapphire should have followed Bradley's comment with something, but they were all temporarily at a loss for what to say.

Mr. Winchester twisted his head to look at the three of them in the back seat, and they all immediately diverted their eyes.

Bradley took the final left turn, which meant they were only about two hundred meters from the emergency room door.

"What's going on?" Mr. Winchester asked, sounding irritated.

"We are taking you to the hospital, Leonardo," Demetrius replied.

"I've told you countless times that I am fine," he said back. "Now turn around and drive me home,"

"Sorry, Mr. Winchester," Bradley told him. "But we care about you too much to do that."

As soon as Bradley's car was beside the ER

door, Peter hopped out and ran inside. Less than a minute later, he and two hospital staff came out.

"Sir," a young ER nurse said to Mr. Winchester. "You have nothing to worry about. We are going to take you in and make sure your heart is shipshape."

"You aren't taking me anywhere," Mr. Winchester replied rudely. "I feel fine."

Since Mr. Winchester's window was open, Peter reached in, unlocked the door, and opened it.

"Mr. Winchester," Peter pleaded. "The doctors and nurses at Stoneburg Memorial are fantastic. They'll run some tests, make sure you are alright, and send you home before you know it."

The other nurse squatted down so she was face-to-face with the now angry (or scared?) elderly man. "The tests and scans we will do are painless," she explained, "and will give the doctors a way to determine the precise cause of your chest pains."

"My chest pains?" he asked, turning around to look at Demetrius. "You promised you would keep that between us."

"Leonardo," Demetrius pleaded sadly. "Please go with these nurses. You can hate me for this later, but—"

"Fine!" Mr. Winchester said loudly, struggling to get out of the car.

The ER staff went to take his arm to help.

"Get your hands off me!" he barked at them. "I'm perfectly capable of walking in on my own."

CHAPTER 22

Shortly after Mr. Winchester was reluctantly whisked away, one of the ER staff suggested that Peter and the rest of them go for dinner and return in a few hours: The hospital expected to have a little more information by then.

* * *

When they got back to the hospital at about half past seven, the nurse called for the physician who had examined Mr. Winchester. The kind doctor explained that Leonardo was doing alright, and that he was slated for a slew of tests the following morning. And the hospital thought it was in everyone's best interests to keep him overnight.

"Would you like to see him?" the doctor asked once she had explained all the specifics and answered all their questions.

"Perhaps it's best if we don't," Demetrius replied. "Meeting us would surely do nothing other than send his blood pressure through the roof."

"Understood," the physician politely replied, handing Sapphire a business card with the direct number to the emergency room desk. "We expect to have the full work-up complete by mid-afternoon tomorrow, but feel free to call anytime if you have any concerns."

"Much appreciated, doctor," Sapphire smiled. "And we apologize for his stubbornness."

"He's nothing compared to some of the people I see," the physician replied. "And you did the right thing by bringing him here: his symptoms are all tell-tale signs of heart disease."

"Thank you, again," Demetrius said, shaking her hand. "We'll come back in the late afternoon tomorrow.

CHAPTER 23

When Bradley pulled into the driveway of Mr. Winchester's home to drop off Demetrius and Sapphire, a worried-looking Zoltan was waiting on the front porch.

"Thank goodness," he said as his parents exited the car. "I was beginning to imagine all sorts of terrible scenarios."

"Everything is fine," his father explained. "We were just dropping Leonardo off at the hospital in Stoneburg."

"Hospital?" Zoltan asked back, having not yet noticed that Mr. Winchester was not with them. "What happened? Was it his heart?"

"Now don't get so worked up, dear," his mother said. "Peter decided we needed to take him there to be looked at. You know, just as a precaution."

"He must be furious," Zoltan commented. "Peter wasn't even supposed to know about his health troubles."

"Someday he'll thank us," Bradley said from

the driver's seat. "Anyway, Pete and I better get going. We'll be back tomorrow at four-ish."

"Drive safely," Zoltan said, waving as they drove away.

* * *

"Pete," Bradley asked when they were about halfway back. "Everything smoothed over with you and Nik?"

"Didn't know there was anything wrong with us in the first place," Peter replied coldly.

"Look," Bradley reacted. "I know it's none of my business. But if something is going on, and you want to talk about it, I'm all ears."

"We are fine," Peter repeated. Then he immediately started counting streetlights as they drove past them. (This was one of the many distraction techniques his psychologist had taught him.)

Bradley knew his brother wasn't being totally honest right now, but forcing the issue would have been senseless.

CHAPTER 24

During lunch on Wednesday, Peter told Nicola everything that was going on with Mr. Winchester. Since she was also fond of the old man, she was concerned about how he was doing.

But when Peter suggested she join them to visit Mr. Winchester after school, she once again came up with "homework" that prevented her from going: this time an English paper. (Now Peter was getting really suspicious...)

* * *

"Leonardo has just dodged a bullet," Dr. Redmond—the cardiologist at Stoneburg Memorial—explained to Peter, Bradley, Zoltan, Demetrius, and Sapphire shortly before five o'clock. "He's going to need a triple by-pass. The arteries around his heart are barely open enough to push blood through. And before you ask, no, there is no way we are going to release him before the surgery."

"Is the operation risky?" Demetrius asked.

"Isn't he too old for such a major procedure?"

"We do heart surgery on much older patients," the polite doctor replied. "We'll do everything we can to ensure your dear friend comes through this fine. Well, not only fine. He'll have his spunk back once those clogged arteries are replaced."

"Have you talked with him about this yet?" Sapphire asked.

"Yes, this morning," the doctor replied. "And let's just say…" Dr. Redmond paused.

"He probably said there was no way he would allow you to operate," Peter commented.

"Yes," the doctor answered, "he is being a little on the stubborn side. But what I can tell you from my twenty years of being a surgeon is this: stubbornness is often the way fear manifests itself."

"But if he refuses to agree to the operation," Zoltan inquired, "then you will be unable to perform it, right?"

"Correct," Dr. Redmond answered. "But I'm quite confident he will change his mind soon. He seemed to be warming up to the idea by the end of our morning chat."

"Let me guess, you threw some statistics at him?" Peter asked.

"How did you know?" the doctor asked right back.

"Because that's exactly what I was going to research when I got home," Peter answered. "But

I guess now I don't have to."

* * *

Mr. Winchester had given them a pretty cold reception, so they decided to head home after a "long and slow" five minutes of near-silence in his hospital room.

* * *

"I suppose I will replace Leonardo, then," Demetrius said during the drive back, "and be Peter's partner at location one."

"Honey," Sapphire said to her husband. "You are far too old to take such an active role in this."

"I'm not much older than Leonardo," he replied.

"I know you want to do what you can," Sapphire said back. "But you have two surgically repaired hips, constant back pain, you're almost deaf in one ear, you have regular migraine headaches, and you're on more medications than I can count."

"Dad!?" Zoltan said in surprise. "You never told me about anything other than the hip replacements and the hearing issue. When did all of—"

"Your father has pride about odd things," Sapphire answered before Demetrius had a chance to. "I'm the only one who knows about all his health issues."

"Health *challenges,*" Demetrius said loudly (and quite rudely!) "And think about it, we have no other options. We certainly can't send Peter on his own."

"Why don't we ask Bridget to help?" Bradley suggested. "Pete, you know she's into puzzles, right? She's also very strong and athletic."

"I don't see why not," Peter replied right away (partially just because he wanted to stop the escalating argument between Zoltan's parents...)

"Tell you what," Bradley said. "After we drop you three off at Mr. Winchester's place, Pete and I will go to Bridget's and ask her."

"Let's go home and grab the DVD first," Peter suggested.

"DVD?" Zoltan asked.

"You don't remember?" Bradley said to Zoltan. "The one from a few years back, of you showing off your powers."

"Looks like I'm not the only one with a failing memory," Demetrius remarked.

CHAPTER 25

When Bradley and Peter showed up unexpectedly at the apartment that Bridget shared with her sister, she happily invited them both in.

"What brings you two to these parts?" Bridget asked in a silly Western accent. "Lose your horses?"

"Sorry to intrude," Peter said. "I'm sure you and your sister—"

"Oh, Becky's out for dinner with friends tonight," Bridget explained. "I haven't eaten yet, actually. Wanna stay? I can whip up some pasta or something, nothing fancy."

It was both a polite and generous offer, but they had to refuse it. Peter and Bradley's mom had a strict rule: If you aren't coming home for dinner, you have to call before five. (That way she wouldn't end up cooking too much.)

Since Peter and Bradley had quite a lot to cover in the next twenty or thirty minutes, they got right to it.

They started by showing her part of the DVD. They were expecting her to think it was a joke or April Fool's prank, but they could see by the expression on her face that she understood it was *real.*

And since Peter knew the most about the whole situation, he did the majority of the talking. Bridget gave Peter her utmost attention the entire time, only stopping him twice to ask for clarification.

"We will totally understand if you prefer not to help," Bradley told her once Peter had finished explaining things. "It's a lot to take in."

"Or if you want to think it over for a couple of days," Peter said, "then that's also cool."

"I'm not sure how much help I can be," she replied. "I mean, I like puzzles and stuff, but I don't know if I could tackle any really hard ones, or—"

"You won't need to *solve* any," Peter told her. "You would just be there, with me, to make any adjustments and changes while *they* are trying to solve the puzzles."

"Adjustments?" she asked.

"Pete," Bradley said, tapping his brother's head. "That sounds confusing to even me, and I already know the plan."

Then he turned to his girlfriend. "What my math-science-whiz brother is trying to say is that you will be there to help him."

Bridget—who had been sitting on the coffee table so she could face them both—leaned in and gave Bradley a kiss. (Boy, did Peter ever feel uncomfortable now!)

"Sure," she said, turning to face Peter. "As long as Brad doesn't get jealous that I'm in a dark cave with you." (Was that comment really necessary, Bridget?)

CHAPTER 26

When Peter arrived home from school on Thursday, his mom told him that he had received a phone call from Stoneburg Memorial.

Peter immediately felt his throat tighten, fearing that his mom was about to inform him of some very bad news.

"The nurse told me," his mom said, "that Mr. Winchester would like you to drop by the hospital for a short visit."

"Oh, okay," Peter replied, feeling immediate relief. "But I guess I'll have to go tomorrow. Brad's got track practice today, and he's my only way there."

"I could drive you," his mom offered. "I'll just bring a book and hang out in the coffee shop down the street."

"You sure?" Peter asked.

"Of course," his mom answered. "That poor old man must be so lonely. Visiting him is the least we can do."

* * *

Knock-knock

"Mr. Winchester, it's me," Peter said as he walked into room 312 of C-wing at Stoneburg Memorial.

"I see you got my message," Mr. Winchester said with a big smile. "I didn't expect you to drop by today, though."

"My mom offered to drive me, and she suggested we come today," he told his elderly friend.

"I guess the apple doesn't fall far from the tree," Mr. Winchester grinned.

"How are you feeling?" Peter asked him.

"Alright, all things considered," he replied. "And I have decided to go ahead with the surgery."

"That's great news," Peter said, giving him a high-five.

"It's scheduled for 9:00 a.m. this coming Monday," Mr. Winchester told Peter. "But let's not talk about that today. The reason I asked you to come is I want an update on how your preparations are progressing."

Peter pulled his chair in close and filled Mr. Winchester in on every detail he could think of. The intelligent old man nodded as he listened, almost as if he were "crossing things off a list" in his head.

"Then I believe it's time to send Sapphire," Mr. Winchester advised. "Let's have her leave tomorrow afternoon."

"That soon?" Peter asked.

"The longer we wait," Mr. Winchester answered, "the bigger Xavier's army gets."

Mr. Winchester picked up a notebook and pen from the bedside table. "Now let's go over everything one more time," he told Peter. "I hope your mom doesn't mind waiting a little longer."

CHAPTER 27

As soon as their last lecture on Friday finished, Bradley and Bridget raced down the main staircase of their college to meet Peter and his friends, who were waiting in the cafeteria.

The group of six quickly crammed into Bradley's car (which had six seat belts, of course!) and went straight to Mr. Winchester's shed.

* * *

Zoltan and his parents were waiting for them, and the spaceship that Sapphire would soon be boarding was in the field behind the shed.

Peter passed an envelope to Sapphire, which contained the note that was going to either "make or break" their plan.

"You still have time to change your mind," Peter told her. "We can always send someone else if you are too nervous or scared."

"I'll be just fine, Peter," she replied. "Demetrius is the worried one here: I don't think he slept a wink last night."

Zoltan had prepared a small supply of snacks and drinks—which he had already put inside the ship's tiny fridge—for his mother to take along on her trip.

"Now, stop looking at me like this is farewell," Sapphire instructed everyone as she stood at the ship's door. "I'll be back before you know it."

"You sure they won't figure out this is all a trick by how you behave?" Neil asked her.

Sapphire started laughing. "I'm a much better actor than you all give me credit for," she said. "I have been pretending, for almost fifty years, that my husband's jokes are funny. And he still hasn't caught on."

"Not funny?" Demetrius reacted. "But you laugh your head off every time I say something entertaining."

"Case and point," Sapphire smiled.

They all gave her a hug, wished her luck, and waved as the door closed. Less than a minute later, the ship was nothing more than a tiny speck in the sky.

CHAPTER 28

Sapphire watched on the crystal clear 360-degree screen as her ship set itself down a couple of kilometers west of Sevlar's capital city. They had decided on these specific landing coordinates because it would guarantee Xavier's troops would have enough time to "catch her" before she attempted to hitchhike into the city.

* * *

The operation Xavier was running was more organized than she had expected: She could see Torin and two others (who she didn't recognize) waiting for her before her vessel had even touched down.

Sapphire double-checked that the note was in her inside jacket pocket—a place that would make them think she was trying to hide it—and then pushed the button to open the door.

"Well, I certainly wasn't expecting limousine service," she joked while exiting the ship. "You must be mistaking me for someone more important."

Torin and his two friends immediately approached Sapphire. "Explain the purpose of your trip!" Torin demanded loudly. (But he also gave her the slightest wink, indicating that he wanted her to play along.)

"Since when does a citizen of Sevlar require a reason to return home?" she asked back boldly.

One of Torin's friends grabbed her wrist, hard. "Turn around!" he yelled. "Now!"

Before she knew it, she had been handcuffed.

"You're coming with us," Torin announced. "And you are not to speak unless we speak to you first. Are we clear?"

"You have no right to—" she started to say.

"Quiet!" one of Torin's friends barked at her, twisting her wrist in a way he knew would cause pain. "Don't make me break your arm, even though I'd love to."

Torin's group then led Sapphire onto their fairly small vessel and instructed her to sit on the floor and face backward.

"And unless you enjoy being hurt," Torin said, "don't turn around."

Sapphire closed her eyes...

* * *

After arriving at the special complex that had been built to imprison Xavier, Sapphire was led off the ship and into a small room with no windows. It could have been compared to a police interrogation room back on Earth. But unlike Earth, this room had no tables or chairs, plus there were no cameras to record what was going on.

These facilities, which were built specifically to hold Xavier (and were "technically" staffed by those loyal to the Sevlarian government) had been severely corrupted. Sapphire guessed that at least half of the people employed here were now on Xavier's payroll.

"Let me tell you how this will work," Torin said loudly, face mere centimeters from hers. "I ask, you answer. If you lie, I hurt you."

"I have nothing to lie about," Sapphire pleaded. "I simply returned to—"

"Lies!" Torin screamed, spraying spit in her face. "Don't make me warn you again. We know who you are, and we know where you came from. Now tell us exactly why you came back to Sevlar by yourself."

"Look, you," Sapphire began. "If you know I am Zoltan and Xavier's mother, and that I am returning from Earth, then what else do you expect me to say?"

One of Torin's helpers got ready to hit her, but Torin waved him off.

"You are obviously here to deliver a message," Torin said to Sapphire. "And no doubt this message is for the lead weather gods. Now tell me exactly what it is you are supposed to be telling them."

"Can't you see how evil Xavier is!?" she yelled. "Why are you letting him do this to you?"

The bigger of Torin's two assistants removed a small steel club from his belt and raised it high.

"Not yet!" Torin said, making sure the thug didn't hit her. "If we knock her out, she can't answer our questions. Come on, let's search her first."

It didn't take them very long to find the note hidden in her jacket pocket.

"What have we here?" Torin asked. "Are you stupid enough to think we wouldn't find this?"

"Do you want me to give an honest answer to that?" she asked sarcastically.

Torin gave her another wink. Then he put his club up to her throat and pretended to push it against her windpipe.

Torin's friends roared with laughter—unaware that this was all an act—and Sapphire intentionally stopped inhaling, which made her face rapidly turn red.

Torin then pushed Sapphire backward, joined in the laughter himself, and got ready to open the note. "Who does Zoltan think is going to help him?" he asked between laughs.

Torin opened the note and read it aloud.

By the time he had finished reading, his expression had changed drastically. "We must take this to Xavier immediately," he told his team.

"Leave her unharmed, for now. Xavier will need to question her more later."

"Now don't forget I am your boss' mother," she told them. "Xavier will kill you if you lay another hand on me."

"Unlikely," Torin laughed. "He would probably give us a raise."

But then Torin winked for the third time. (He had obviously figured out the hidden message!)

CHAPTER 29

"Did they actually think my mother could get this note to the lead weather gods undetected?" Xavier remarked while scanning its contents from the bed in his cell. "The fools!"

"And to think your brother would risk his own mother's life," Torin added, laughing along, "just goes to show how much of an imbecile he is."

"We should send a few people to these three locations, now," one of the henchmen suggested, "before they have a chance to finish getting ready for us."

"Indeed we should," Xavier agreed. "The sooner, the better."

"And what do you want us to do with your mother?" the other assistant asked.

Xavier didn't respond straight away. (Was there some affection hidden behind all that evilness?)

"I think I have an idea," Torin began. "May I?"

"By all means," Xavier replied, keen to hear

more.

"Zoltan, Leonardo, and the rest of them will likely change their plan if Sapphire doesn't return soon," he explained. "I'd be willing to bet they have a *plan B* ready."

"But we can't send her back," Xavier commented.

"Not alone," Torin went on, "but I could *escort* her back."

"I'm not following you," Xavier said.

"I can pretend to be an ally of the lead weather gods," Torin told his boss. "And use these two lies: One, I'll tell them I was given the duty to escort Sapphire safely back to Earth. And two, I'll say that I am the first of many weather gods being sent to assist."

"This is sounding better by the minute," Xavier smiled.

"But what's preventing her from blurting everything out the minute you two arrive on Earth?" one assistant asked.

"There is nothing that Sapphire would regret more than being the one responsible for children getting harmed," Torin said while rubbing his hands together. "I will threaten her with this: If she so much as whispers one word about what's going on, I harm Peter and his friends."

"Torin," Xavier commended his faithful follower, "I made the right decision when I appointed you to your current position. You are doing me proud."

"It is my honor to serve you," Torin lied.

"What will you do once you are there?" Xavier questioned him.

"I will reassure them that help is on the way," he answered. "And that all those yet to arrive will be going directly to the three locations."

"So they'll rush to each spot, thinking help is on the way," Xavier said in a sinister voice. "When it's my troops who are coming."

"Exactly," Torin smiled. "They'll be sitting ducks."

"Depart as soon as you can," Xavier told Torin. "I will start assembling a team to send to Earth a day or two behind you."

"In a few days from now," Torin grinned. "You will finally possess the amulet."

"And then the fun can really begin!" Xavier bellowed.

CHAPTER 30

In less than an hour, Torin and Sapphire were aboard Leonardo's ship. As badly as she wanted to speak candidly with him, they both kept up the facade, as they couldn't be sure they weren't being listened to.

* * *

Once the ship was out of Sevlar's stratosphere, Torin let out a big sigh.

"I can't believe we pulled that off," he said to Sapphire. "I was worried Xavier was going to send someone along with us."

"Thank goodness that's not the case," Sapphire agreed. Then she lowered her voice. "Are you sure it's safe to talk?"

"We are perfectly fine now," Torin answered. "Sevlar employs a planetary shield. You know, the one that blocks all radio waves from penetrating. It was built to, well, keep Selvar off the maps. It makes our planet appear uninhabited."

"Come to think of it," Sapphire commented. "I

kind of remember learning that in grade school."

"I suppose just like any other historical fact," Torin laughed, "it's only interesting to a few select people. Everyone else probably just slept through that class. But before I forget, let's get your announcement out."

"Announcement?" Sapphire asked, a little confused.

"The one hidden in the note," Torin replied. "Leonardo did a great job of concealing that message."

"Actually," Sapphire said, "Peter wrote it. But he didn't explain exactly how he had hidden it."

"Well, Xavier has the actual paper now," Torin told her. "But before I handed it to him, I went to a washroom and copied it down on some toilet paper."

Dear Lead Weather Gods,

I'm sending this message to you, via the trusted hands of Sapphire, as I fear Xavier's army may come here soon and attempt to steal the amulet. Unfortunately, I don't think we can hold them off on our own. We need help, and you are our second-to-last option. Everything I've written here, from the next line on, will explain what we are planning, and exactly what we need you to do:

We will be hiding the amulet.

And we desperately need help protecting it.

I am including 3 sets of coordinates on this page.

Please send whoever you can to these spots, to help us fight.

And send them before it's too late.

With enough on our side, we can hold Xavier off.

But without help, our chances are slim.

And the consequences of losing are huge.

Loyally yours,

Leonardo

52°44'2"N   7°14'48"W
31°35'49"N   34°54'2"E
29°3'42"N   119°11'3"E

HI READER! (^_^)
TAKE ANOTHER STAB AT SPOTTING THE
HIDDEN MESSAGE!

"Look at the start of the note, where it says *the second-to-last option,*" Torin explained. "That phrase made absolutely no sense. And the other thing that was a dead giveaway was the phrase *from the next line on.*"

Sapphire shook her head.

"Here's what those two things were telling me," Torin continued. "Starting from the *We will be hiding* line, I was supposed to use the *second-last letter* of each sentence. It spelled out the message they wanted me to pick up on."

Sapphire looked at the note again and said what those nine letters spelled.

Eight Fig Rd

"That's Leonardo's address," she smiled.

"Yes," Torin replied. "I knew that meant he wanted me to send out a distress call to some of my friends, and tell them to go directly to Leonardo's home."

"Do you think anyone will come?" Sapphire asked. "I mean, they must all be terrified of Xavier."

"Luckily, I have at least a few friends who still

have strong morals," Torin said. "As long as they are close enough to get to Earth, some will help."

"I'd better zip my lip and let you get that message out," Sapphire said.

* * *

Ten minutes later, the S.O.S. had been successfully broadcast to eleven of Torin's closest friends, all of whom were managing planets less than a day's journey from Earth.

But how many of those eleven would show up?

CHAPTER 31

When Peter walked through Mr. Winchester's front door at seven thirty on Saturday morning, he was surprised to see not only that Sapphire had safely returned, but that there were three new faces as well.

"Welcome back," Peter said while giving her a big hug. "I guess the note worked, eh?"

"Brilliantly," Sapphire replied. "And please allow me to do the introductions: Peter, this is Torin, Gabriella, and Theo."

Torin ran over to shake Peter's hand. "I am truly honored," he said to Peter. "You are a legend on my planet."

Gabriella and Theo also shook hands with the red-faced teenager: the first Earthling they had ever met. They too commended Peter on all the hard work and ingenuity that he continually put into keeping Earth safe.

Somewhat uncomfortably, Peter asked, "Are there, uh... any *more* weather gods coming?"

"Only time will tell," Demetrius replied from the big rocking chair—Mr. Winchester's usual spot—"Torin, why don't you explain."

Peter listened intently to Torin describe how he had managed to dupe Xavier and get Sapphire back safely. Torin also said he was hopeful that at least a couple more weather gods would arrive to help.

Although having nine or ten weather gods on their side would have been ideal, three would suffice: That way they could send one with each team. It also meant Zoltan and Demetrius could "hover" and assist wherever necessary.

"Brad and everyone else are going to get here at nine, which is pretty soon," Peter told his audience of supernatural beings. "I only came this early because I was so anxious to know if there was any news."

"You could have just called," Zoltan commented.

Peter smiled. "I know," he said. "But if you had told me on the phone there *was* news, I would have ridden here so fast that I probably would have disregarded numerous traffic laws. And we certainly don't want that!"

* * *

By shortly past ten, Bradley, Neil, Nicola, Claire, and Bridget had all been briefed on the current state of this constantly evolving plan. Peter had decided to put Gabriella with Neil and

Nicola, Theo with Claire and Bradley, and have Torin team up with himself and Bridget.

Since Zoltan and his parents had completely set up the challenges at all three locations, they concluded that now was the right time to send the teams to those spots, where they would wait for whoever was coming...

CHAPTER 32

"You three are my most talented, dedicated, and capable followers," Xavier said through the bars of his cell. "That's why I'm putting this crucial task in your hands."

Maximillian, Cynthia, and Aurora—who felt honored to be entrusted with something so important—were both nervous and eager to hear what was next.

"My baby brother," he went on, "who you know has turned into a constant headache for me, has allowed his stupidity to present us with an opportunity to snatch the amulet from under his nose.

"You have each received an envelope, which contains the specific longitude and latitude of where you are to go. One of those three locations is where the amulet is being hidden. We have no intel on which is the most likely, so we are going to hit all three at the same time.

"They don't think we'll be coming for weeks, or

even months. So we have an opportunity, right now, to catch them off guard. And just in case you were wondering, I am giving you full authorization..." Xavier paused and started laughing. "Well, I suppose I don't have the official capacity to make executive decisions, do I?" He laughed even harder. "But since I will soon be the leader of the entire universe, I have no qualms about saying things like this: You may, and are highly encouraged, to do *everything necessary* to get that amulet. In other words, I don't care how many people die."

CHAPTER 33

Zoltan (with the help of the amulet's powers) decided to deliver the team of Neil, Nicola, and Gabriella first.

* * *

When they arrived at their location—which was the hottest of the three spots—they prepared to enter the ancient and mystical-looking place where they would be attempting to trap as many evil weather gods as possible.

"How did people thousands of years ago tolerate this heat?" Neil commented. "It's too hot to even think."

"C'mon," Nicola said. "It's not that hot. And the humidity here is next to zero."

"As soon as we enter the ruins," Gabriella mentioned, "you'll completely forget about the heat. I bet it's comfortably cool inside."

* * *

"Kind of feels weird doing this stuff without Pete, doesn't it?" Neil innocently asked Nicola, completely unaware that things between her and Peter were not one hundred percent rosy.

"You are always giving him way too much credit," she responded. "I mean, I know he's smart, but we are also capable of doing almost all of these things without him."

Neil, unfortunately, didn't pick up on the nuance of what she was saying. He made the poor choice of asking another question, "But you'd feel way safer with him around, wouldn't you?"

"Safer?" she asked back. "Pete's not capable of defending himself, let alone us."

"Neil, Nicola," Gabriella said loudly, clearly not interested in letting this conversation continue any further. "Which one of you has the instructions for this challenge? You know, the note Peter wrote and put in an envelope?"

"That would be me," Neil replied, removing it from his hideously untidy backpack.

"Place it on the floor, right over there," she instructed Neil. "That way whoever enters will notice it immediately, pick it up, and find it contains instructions for this challenge."

"Pete sure did think of everything," Neil said while putting it where she was pointing.

"Why do you keep talking about Pete like he's some kind of god?" Nicola asked, sounding agitated again.

Neil finally put two and two together. (But how could Nicola and Peter be in the middle of a rough patch? They were supposed to be, like, the perfect couple...)

CHAPTER 34

Zoltan had just returned from dropping off the second team—Claire, Bradley, and Theo—and was now taking a breather before departing with the third and final group.

"We know the amulet amplifies your powers significantly," Peter said to him. "But doesn't that also intensify how tired you feel during and after using it?"

"I've never given that any thought," Zoltan replied. "It's like comparing apples and oranges. But now that you mention it, I certainly do take a long nap on the days I use it."

"Cool, so it does amplify everything," Peter said. "Anyway, not to worry, I was just curious; The scientific part of my brain just wants to understand exactly how it works."

"Even though having supernatural abilities goes against everything you were taught in science class?" Demetrius asked, laughing a little.

"Because it goes against everything," Peter

replied.

* * *

Peter was astonished by how smooth the ride was as Zoltan flew him and his team to their location. It was almost like Zoltan had created some type of *invisible wind-proof bubble* around his group. Even though they were technically traveling at twenty-two times the speed of sound, it felt like they were completely stationary.

* * *

"Thank you for flying with Zoltan aviation," Zoltan joked right after setting them down just outside the entrance to the caves. "We look forward to serving you again."

Peter felt a little dizzy and out of it: like the feeling that someone gets when disembarking from a multi-day sailing trip. He quickly pinched his forearm to make sure he wasn't dreaming!

As soon as Zoltan had wished them good luck and set off back for Clearville, Bridget, Torin, and Peter took themselves on a small tour of the caves. They wanted to ensure that Zoltan had set things up exactly as Peter had outlined.

"This place is eerie," Bridget said to Peter while walking through the dark and chilly tunnels.

"No kidding," Peter replied. "I hope we don't have to spend more than a day or two here."

"I would suspect," Torin commented, "that whoever is coming will arrive sometime later today. When Xavier smells opportunity, he doesn't hesitate."

"How many traps do we have here?" Peter asked Torin (having forgotten to get that important detail from Zoltan earlier.)

"Not sure," he replied. "I was assuming you and Zoltan had decided on that ahead of time."

* * *

"Looks like there are four in total," Bridget said once their inspection was complete. "But, uh... what do we do while we wait?"

"Guess we just pull up a seat on a rock," Peter replied (not having an answer to that question.)

"Don't suppose you brought any puzzles or games?" Bridget jokingly asked.

"I only wish," Peter answered right away. A few seconds later, he remembered something. "Maybe I do have a cool way for us to kill time. I've still got that riddle Mr. Winchester wrote for me several days ago. Well, technically my math teacher has the original riddle in her desk, but let's not get into why... Anyway, I remembered it quite clearly, so I wrote it down. Wanna try to figure it out?"

"Stupid question," she smiled. "Come on, let's see, let's see!"

Torin also came closer. (Sevlarians were born puzzlers, so his curiosity was piqued.)

Peter passed the envelope to Bridget.

Mrs. Waterton, a kind and caring mother and grandmother, loved baking for her family. She especially liked making cookies, as they were her grandchildren's favorite.

Early in the morning of her eldest granddaughter Emily's twelfth birthday, she baked a huge batch, knowing the smile it would bring to Emily's face. Emily came downstairs even before her parents had woken up, as the wonderful smell had drifted up to her room.

At her spot at the table, there was a plate with four freshly baked cookies on it.

After receiving a big birthday hug, she sat down and got ready to devour this special treat.

Just before Emily was about to grab a cookie, her grandmother said she had prepared a little birthday game.

She told her granddaughter that she had folded up a ten-dollar bill, and hidden it under one of the chocolate *chip cookies. If Emily could guess which cookie it was under on her first try, she would not only get that ten dollars, but also an extra ten as well.*

Emily pointed at one of the four cookies. Her grandmother lifted it, unveiling the folded bill!

Emily was now twenty dollars richer! What a birthday!

But how did she know which cookie it was under?

HI READER! (^_^)
READY TO TAKE A STAB AT THIS RIDDLE?

Bridget was wiping away tears with her shirt sleeve when she finished the last part of the note.

Peter looked at Torin, and they both shrugged their shoulders.

"Are you feeling okay?" Peter asked her.

"Oh, sorry," she replied, forcing a smile through her tears. "This riddle just made me remember my mom: She used to make the most amazing chocolate chip cookies."

"You haven't met your mother in a while?" Torin asked, unaware that Bridget's parents had passed away a couple years ago in a car accident.

This, of course, caused her to start crying quite hard. Peter knew Bridget needed a hug right now. The instant he went to hug her, Bridget wrapped her arms around Peter tightly and sobbed on his shoulder.

"It's okay," Peter told her, patting her lightly on the back.

* * *

Peter was preparing to put the riddle back in his bag, as he wanted to spare Bridget any more emotional distress.

"Avoiding the subject of my parents' deaths doesn't make it hurt any less," she told Peter and Torin. "Now get that riddle back out, let's take a crack at it right now. And I think I have a way to make this a little more fun: How about we wager on who can solve it first? We each put in a dollar, winner takes all. You guys in?"

Peter—aka Mr. overly prepared—took out three pencils and three sheets of paper. "Probably best if we give each other space," he suggested. Then he started laughing. "Well, at least give *me* some space. I talk to myself non-stop when I'm thinking. And if either of you is too close, you might overhear me say the answer."

"A big know-it-all, eh?" Bridget joked, lightly slugging Peter in the shoulder. "What makes you think one of *us* won't figure it out first?"

Bridget read it aloud for a second time, and then passed the paper back to Peter.

* * *

Less than five minutes after splitting up to individually contemplate the solution, Torin announced, "I think I got it!"

"Unlikely," Bridget laughed, looking up from her *still blank* sheet of paper. "But let's hear anyway."

They quickly congregated in the middle.

"The folded-up bill," Torin began, "was easy to spot because the cookie on top of it was too small."

"You mean, like," Peter asked, "the corners were sticking out?"

"Exactly," Torin replied.

"Theoretically," Bridget reacted, "that could be a solution. But I doubt that's it. The riddle said it was *hiding* under one of the cookies."

"I think I agree with Bridget," Peter added. "If the corners of the bill could be seen, that wouldn't constitute hiding."

"Fair enough," Torin said. "You guys come up with anything?"

"Not yet," Bridget replied. "But I'm working on something."

"I do have a guess," Peter said. "But I think I have an unfair advantage here: I read this riddle about a week ago."

"Then give us five more minutes," Bridget suggested. "If Torin or I still haven't come up with the solution, then we'll hear your idea."

"Cool," Peter agreed.

* * *

"Five minutes are up," Peter said. "Any guesses?"

They gathered together again.

"Torin, you can go first," Bridget encouraged him.

"Alright," Torin smiled. "Cookies are fairly light. And a bill would have to be folded at least three times to make it small enough to hide under a cookie. Emily could see that one of the four cookies was sitting a little higher up on the plate."

"Well, that was much better than your first attempt, "Bridget smiled, "but I'm not giving that answer *the OK.*"

"Then I guess there's no point in telling you my idea," Peter followed, "as that was pretty much the premise of what I was thinking."

"Then," Bridget grinned, "allow me to educate you boys."

HI READER! (^_^)
WHAT DO YOU THINK? ANY IDEAS?

"You were both assuming," she continued, "that Emily had to choose one of the FOUR cookies. But..." She paused, and looked back and forth at Peter and Torin, trying to gauge if that clue had helped. "But nowhere in the riddle did it say that all four cookies were chocolate chip. It only said that the bill was hidden under *one of the chocolate chip cookies.* Two of the four cookies were chocolate chip, and the other two were something else."

"But that still doesn't explain how she knew which of those two it was under," Peter commented.

"I can explain that as well," Bridget proudly continued. "One of the two chocolate chip cookies was significantly smaller than the other: so small that it could never have hidden a bill. The only place that the 10-dollar bill could have been was under the bigger of the two chocolate chip ones."

No reaction. (Well, other than the *Why didn't I see that?* look on their faces.)

"Nicely done," Peter told Bridget, giving her a high-five. "Neither of those things even crossed my mind."

"Me neither," Torin added. "But I can say this: I would sure love to find out what chocolate chip cookies taste like. There is no such thing as chocolate on Sevlar."

"You Sevlarians are missing out!" Bridget joked.

CHAPTER 35

"How long have we been here?" Bradley impatiently asked Claire and Theo. "Feels like forever."

"A little over two hours," Theo replied. He was currently sitting on a folding chair in front of the TV monitors.

"No sense in pacing around," Claire advised Bradley. "You know how the saying goes: a watched pot never boils."

"I agree with her on that," Theo added. "Besides, we have high-quality cameras installed outside the entrance, all of which are equipped with very sensitive motion detectors. The instant someone gets near these caves, a silent alarm will be triggered, and that red light mounted on the center TV will start flashing."

* * *

Although Bradley was never officially diagnosed with ADHD, his parents had had their suspicions, as Bradley had never been able to sit still. When he was in Grade 2, his mom and dad were asked to meet with his teacher. (Bradley was apparently getting up from his desk numerous times during class.)

Since Bradley was their first child, they didn't think or worry too much about it; They just figured excess energy was responsible for this inability to stay seated. They quickly signed him up for all sorts of after school programs, all sports related. They were hoping this would give him the opportunity he needed to get a portion of this restlessness out of his system.

To everyone's pleasure, Bradley seemed to somewhat settle down in school over the next few weeks. That was sufficient enough evidence for everyone (teacher included) to "falsely conclude" that the lack of physical activity had been to blame.

* * *

"Hey, Brad," Claire—who was starting to get a little irritated watching Bradley's pacing—said. "You hear about Pete and Nik?"

Bradley was an excellent actor, so when he replied with, "No, why?" she completely believed him.

"It's not like they're fighting or anything," she told Bradley. "But I have a feeling they aren't going to be a couple much longer."

"You're playing me, right?" Bradley said. "Those two are over the moon about each other."

"Were over the moon," Claire said. "Until Travis started to—"

"Travis Penner?" Bradley asked loudly. "The captain of the volleyball and tennis teams?"

"Yup, you got it," she said. "Not to mention one of the cutest guys in the whole school."

"But he's two years older than her," Bradley said. "That's not cool. He should go for someone his own age."

"Actually," Claire explained. "He's only five and a half months older than Nik. And I only found this next detail out a few days ago, but Travis is so smart that he skipped kindergarten."

"How does someone skip kindergarten?" Bradley asked doubtfully.

"Rumor has it," Claire said, "that he was pretty much able to teach all the other kids in his kindergarten class everything he was supposed to be learning. So after his first week, the school bumped him up to Grade 1."

"I guess both Neil and Pete are in the market for new girlfriends then, eh?" Bradley remarked (catching Claire by surprise!)

Claire got ready to yell at Bradley about how insensitive and unnecessary that comment was, but right before she opened her mouth, the red light began flashing...

CHAPTER 36

"Peter! Bridget!" Torin said loudly while running over to them. "Someone just arrived at Claire, Brad, and Theo's location!"

He showed them the message displayed on his very futuristic-looking, palm-sized TV screen.

"Does it say how many?" Peter asked right away.

"Unfortunately, no," Torin answered. "But they'll let us know as soon as they can."

"Then odds are someone will show up here pretty soon, right?" Bridget asked.

"Most likely," Torin replied.

* * *

"Guys, look!" Peter said a few minutes later, pointing at the TV monitors.

Not only was the little red light now flashing, but they could clearly see someone was walking toward the entrance.

Much to their surprise (and pleasure) there was only one figure approaching. But he was no stranger at all... Maximillian!

* * *

"Imbeciles!" Maximillian laughed while walking toward the caves. "I still can't believe they thought their whiny note to the lead weather gods would save their skin." Once inside, he waited a few seconds while his eyes adjusted to the relative darkness. "Please tell me the amulet is here, and not at one of the other two locations. Whoever hands it over to Xavier will surely become his second-in-command."

Weather gods don't require potions or elixirs to command the wind and rain, but they do need to use their hands to perform these feats. So just to be safe, Maximillian proceeded with both arms in the ready position while walking through the tunnel and into the large chamber.

Maximillian was no doofus: He knew getting the amulet would involve more than simply *walking through a couple tunnels,* but even he was surprised when he saw a note laying on the floor.

"Well, looks like I get to have a little fun after all," he said to himself, knowing full well the note would contain some sort of riddle or clue.

In addition to the note, this large chamber also had an old clock mounted on the wall just inside the entrance, a bow and quiver full of arrows leaning against the wall, and a yellow line painted on the floor (which was also close to the

133

entrance.) And there appeared to be something at the far end of the chamber, but there wasn't enough natural light coming in to see it clearly.

The amulet you have come to retrieve is not something that any average weather god deserves to possess. Only the cleverest of the clever...

On the ground, beside the bow and arrows, there is a battery-powered flashlight. If you shine it across the chamber, you will see a target, which looks very much like a dartboard.

Before reading on, Maximillian picked up the flashlight and turned it on. Now he could see the target easily: In the center of it, where the bullseye would usually be, there was an X.

Task: Get one of the arrows in the X

Rules: You must stand behind the yellow line. (And just in case you miss the target with all 25 arrows, you are permitted to pick them up and reuse them as many times as you need to.)

Maximillian was from a very well-off family, so he was no stranger to the fine sport of archery.

But on Sevlar, archery's roots were not from hunting; It had always been strictly a *sport for the rich,* similar to the status polo has in the United Kingdom.

"What a flimsy and pathetic bow," he said while lifting it up and inspecting it. "How can they possibly shoot arrows straight with something as weak as this?"

He placed one arrow in position and pulled the string back.

"And talk about a loose string," he laughed. "I fired tauter bows than this when I was barely old enough to walk."

Maximillian was one of the top five archers on Sevlar, and had even won the annual competition three times in the past five years.

His first shot, although fairly straight, didn't even make it two-thirds of the way across the chamber.

"This is going to take a little getting used to," he complained.

* * *

By the time he shot his fifteenth arrow, he had become fairly accustomed to the trajectory and speed. Plus, he had been able to determine that the relative weakness of the bow meant he had to aim a reasonable distance above the target, as its flight path was parabolic.

"Not bad," he commended himself, having finally hit the outside ring of the target. "Just a little more tweaking here and there of my positioning, and I should be able to hit that stupid X."

* * *

Unbeknownst to Maximillian, Peter's team had been watching him from the instant he had arrived. Whoever had built these catacombs had also carved a narrow path adjacent to the chamber, with a few baseball-size holes in the wall: which were likely made so people could keep an eye on whatever took place in the chamber.

* * *

Frustrated that he hadn't hit the X on his first round, Maximillian took the empty quiver and started picking up the arrows. A few of them were unusable now, as the heads had snapped off when they hit the hard rock instead of the soft target.

While doing this, he noticed the outline of a door around the target itself.

"Ah, I see," he commented. "I hit the bullseye, it opens the door."

Maximillian may have been a skilled archer, but he was an extremely impatient individual. For his second round of shots, he was spending less and less time lining up each one, hence more and more of the arrows were off target.

"Blast them!" he yelled in frustration, throwing the bow down hard (like a bratty child who didn't get his way) when he noticed the quiver was once again empty.

* * *

He only had twelve usable arrows left.

"Earth folks can't even construct the simplest of things properly," he mumbled.

* * *

Torin was finding this so entertaining that he had to walk away from his viewing spot for a minute. Peter and Bridget both also felt like laughing, but were able to contain themselves.

* * *

On his third round, Maximillian's ninth arrow seemed to hit right on the border of the tiny circle containing the X.

"Oh, come on!" he yelled. "It's in the X!"

He stormed across the chamber to examine the arrow's placement.

"Over fifty percent of this is in the bullseye," he complained loudly. "That door should be open!"

In a rage, he yanked the arrow out. Still holding it tightly in his hand, he jabbed it hard into the center of the X.

"This technically isn't cheating," he said. "I already hit the stupid bullseye. Their pathetic contraption is just malfunctioning."

But nothing happened.

His anger escalated, and he proceeded to jab three more arrows into the X, yelling and whining when the door still didn't open.

* * *

Peter and Bridget had to take a break from watching as they could not contain their laughter any longer. Seeing such a capable and (supposedly) mature supernatural being throw a temper tantrum was way too amusing.

* * *

Maximillian pulled all four arrows out, stuffed them back into the quiver, and stomped back to the line.

"There must be some sort of fail-safe in place," he scowled, "that doesn't permit the door to open unless I'm standing back by the entrance when an arrow hits the target."

Then he paused, closed his eyes, and took a few slow, deep breaths. He got the bow in position, opened his aiming eye, and lightly put an arrow in place.

This shot was a gold medal winner: It sailed beautifully and landed dead-center in the *X*.

"It's been a pleasure," he bragged, bowing to his non-existent audience.

But when he looked up, the door hadn't budged.

"This is asinine!" he yelled. "They have created a challenge that cannot be won!"

His face hardened. "I've had enough of their silly games."

He got his hands ready to conjure up an enormous blast of wind.

He sent air hard at the far wall, expecting it to blow the door open. The stone door didn't move at all, but the target went flying off the wall.

The angered Maximillian ran over and picked it up. "There's no way hitting the *X* would have opened the door," he whined. "The target was not connected to anything."

He chucked the useless target, and it busted in half when it hit the wall.

Maximillian looked at the broken target, the scattered arrows, and then back toward the entrance. The hands on the clock showed it was now 4:25, meaning he had now been here for close to thirty minutes.

But as he shuffled toward the yellow line, something clicked. He reread part of the note.

Get one of the arrows in the X.

He looked up at the clock again (but not to check the time.)

"I can't believe I fell for that," he said, shaking his head.

Maximillian's eyes were focused on one specific spot of the out-of-place-and-totally-unnecessary clock: The Roman numeral for the number ten.

"There's my *X,*" he said, cracking a bit of a smile. "Many wall clocks, especially older ones on Earth, use Roman numerals instead of numbers. And the Roman numeral for ten is *X.*"

He pulled out one of the arrows and jammed it into the clock's *X*.

He saw the area around the *X* (which was some kind of button) displace back into the clock a little.

"They won't be fooling me again," he stated. Then he turned around to see the stone door slowly opening.

CHAPTER 37

"Guys!" Gabriella said to Nicola and Neil while running over with her communicator in hand. "Peter's group has company! Max is there!"

"Max?" Neil asked. "You mean Maximillian? By himself?"

"I think so," Gabriella answered. "But I can't say for sure. Torin's message was very brief."

"Then someone is gonna show up here, like, really soon," Nicola said, sounding worried.

"You have nothing to fear, Nicola," Gabriella said, hoping to reassure her. "We are more than ready."

* * *

"Look!" Nicola yelled, getting up from her chair and walking to the monitor. "Someone's approaching!"

"Is that who I think it is?" Neil said in shock, as the figure was now close enough to the camera to make out her face.

"Cynthia?" Nicola gasped, having just made

the same deduction as Neil.

"Is she alone?" Gabriella asked, unable to see the screens that were being unintentionally blocked by her two teenage teammates.

"Yeah, just her," Neil told her. "I guess we should consider ourselves lucky that she didn't bring any friends."

"Very lucky," Gabriella said, correcting Neil.

* * *

Cynthia had never been one to feel any sort of fear or apprehension. (Or if she did, she certainly never let it show.) She strode into the entrance as if it was the front door of her own home.

She was forced to stop briefly, as her eyes needed a few seconds to adjust to the lack of light. Once her pupils had dilated enough to make out where she was, she spotted the envelope on the ground.

"You must be kidding me," she said, picking up the note like it was a nuisance rather than an intriguing puzzle. Then she allowed herself to smile, but only just a little. "I suppose it can't hurt to have a little fun before I walk out with the amulet."

> *Like any other priceless item, the amulet has to be kept somewhere safe, in a spot that only a brilliant mind can get to. Is that, by any chance, you?*

She wanted to rip the paper in half after reading those lines, but knew the remainder of the note would contain instructions necessary for her puzzle.

> *Task: Roll the steel bowling ball (which is heavier than it looks!) across this room, into the hole on the far side. (The hole is about twice the diameter of the ball, so your aim had better be perfect!)*
>
> *Rules: Both feet must be inside the yellow square when you roll it. (The hole closes when you are not standing in the square.)*

"Should be easy," she said. "I bet that brat Peter came up with this one." She crushed the paper and dropped it on the ground. "A moronic game created by a moronic boy."

As indicated in the note, the ball was quite heavy. And it was different than a regulation 10-pin bowling ball, as it had no finger holes.

Guess I'll have to do a Granny shot to roll this thing," she remarked.

She took her position in the small square; She could barely spread her feet wide enough to swing the ball back between her legs.

"And that daft boy was too stupid to even make this square a decent size," she complained.

The floor wasn't polished smooth, but it was relatively flat. As long as she rolled it straight, and with the correct amount of force, getting it in the hole was certainly possible.

Her first attempt was horrifically off-target, which was obvious from the instant she released the ball. It was so bad that she didn't even bother watching its trajectory, all she did was curse and kick at the air.

Since there was only one ball, she was going to have to walk over and pick it up after each attempt. (Just one more thing to drive up her level of irritation...)

* * *

Gabriella, Neil, and Nicola were watching this unravel on the TV monitors. (Zoltan had installed a couple of cameras—in very inconspicuous spots—in the large chamber.)

"She needs to chill out," Neil laughed. "That's not good for her blood pressure."

"What do you know about blood pressure?" Nicola asked, sounding a little bothered.

"Who peed in your cornflakes?" Neil jokingly said to Nicola. (That was an expression his mom regularly used when he was being standoffish.)

"Can't you just keep quiet for one minute, and focus on what you are supposed to?" she barked at Neil. "Has no one ever told you that ninety-nine percent of what comes out of your mouth is complete gibberish?"

(Yikes! Maybe Neil shouldn't have made that cornflakes comment...)

* * *

Cynthia took her time to line up for her second roll, as she didn't feel like doing this silly and childish game for any longer than was absolutely necessary.

"Okay, Mr. Ball," she grumbled. "Go find your way into that blasted hole."

She rolled it a little softer than she should have, but her aim was magnificent this time.

"Not bad for a beginner," she said, complimenting herself and getting ready to step out of the square the instant the ball stopped. But a few meters before it reached the hole, it began curving to the left.

"Gimme a break," she whined, reverting to her bad mood. "I have to factor in a sloped floor as well?"

For her third roll, she deliberately aimed it a little to the right, and also added some more velocity. She was using this attempt as a way to determine exactly how much she needed to compensate for the uneven surface.

It began curving to the left at roughly the same spot as before, and was about 50 centimeters left of the hole when it eventually rolled past it.

"I'll have to compensate a little more," she

complained, angrily picking it up again.

She elected to give it a little less juice this time, as her previous roll had gone further than she expected.

"Let's see if that does the trick," she said right after releasing the ball. She had no way of knowing if she had calculated things perfectly, but was reasonably confident that it would be at least somewhere close.

But instead of curving left, the ball curved right this time!

"Oh, please," she said loudly, not even waiting for the ball to stop before stepping out of the square. "Didn't whoever construct this chamber have a level?"

* * *

Watching all this play out was turning out to be quite entertaining for Neil and Gabriella. Nicola, on the other hand, wasn't even looking at the monitors. (Neil knew she would likely snap at him again if he made any comment, so he kept his mouth shut.)

* * *

Cynthia was now lying on her stomach, one eye shut, looking in the direction she was planning to roll this dreadful ball. As much as she wanted to be able to tell herself she had worked out where the imperfections on the floor were, her naked eye had not been up to that task.

"Wish I'd brought chalk," she said under her breath. "Then I could probably mark a path a little better."

She aimed the ball halfway between her two previous attempts, figuring that gave her the best chance of success.

Another right curve.

She tried again, slightly more to the left.

Right curve, again.

She lined up once more, ever more slightly to the left.

A third consecutive right curve.

"Hold on," she said loudly, fairly confused. "Now that one should definitely have curved left. This doesn't make any sense."

To test out her theory that something was off, she aimed directly at the hole this time, knowing it would curve left (just like it had the first time she rolled it straight for the hole.)

But it curved right!

"This is ridiculous!" she yelled. "Is this a

floating floor or something?"

* * *

Neil was having way too much fun right now: He was laughing so hard he had tears in his eyes, and his face was bright red. "Wouldn't be surprised if she tried throwing it next," he said.

* * *

All Cynthia could think to do next (other than say a whole pile of Sevlarian swear words) was to go up and very closely examine the area in front of the hole.

She placed the heavy ball on the floor about three meters before the hole—which was now closed since she wasn't standing in the square—roughly the location where it always started to curve. Since she didn't have anything to write with, she put a pebble on the ground to mark where she was rolling it from.

She gave it a soft push, and watched it curve to the right as it rolled.

Then she moved about ten centimeters to the left of the pebble and tried again. She kept moving to the left, little by little, but every single time the ball curved right.

She carried the ball—which she had quickly grown to despise—back to the yellow square, stepped inside it, and aimed about fifty centimeters to the left of the hole: This had to work.

This time the ball curved left!

Now Cynthia was fuming. Taking long and powerful strides, she went over and picked up the ball. It looked like she was about to heave it at the stone door (she probably wanted to!), but she elected to redirect her anger at something more meaningful.

"Time to get to the bottom of this," she said after a few deep breaths. "I need to figure out what's making the ball change directions. It can't be the floor."

She held the ball with two hands and stood right above the closed hole. Carrying the ball, she walked over to the right wall. But nothing about it looked unique.

She didn't feel like holding this heavy steel ball any longer than was necessary, so she walked over to the left wall next.

The closer she got to the left wall, the more obvious it became.

HI READER!
WHAT DID CYNTHIA JUST FIGURE OUT?

"Cynthia, Cynthia, the brilliant, beautiful, bashful Cynthia," she said to herself. "Looks like you have just outsmarted them. But I suppose I should be happy I was sent here alone. It would have been embarrassing for anyone to see how long it took me."

She put the ball down, took a deep breath, and looked like she was going to announce something.

"Hey! Wherever you are!" she called out at the top of her lungs. (Did she know she was being watched?) "I have figured out your stupid trick. You are using magnets to change the path of this steel ball. The only thing I haven't pinpointed yet is how you are switching the magnet from the left wall to the right wall and back."

Cynthia began inspecting both walls, very carefully this time.

But there was nothing of importance to note...

"Maybe *they* don't control the magnets," she asked herself. "Maybe *I* do?"

She started pacing around.

"But how could I be triggering the magnets to shift?" she asked herself. "Or is there something I have been doing, without even knowing, that has been switching them?"

She continued walking around.

And around some more.

Then (for no obvious reason) she looked down at her feet. (Her feet?)

"Oh," she smiled. "Very clever."

She picked up the ball and bolted back to the square.

"The only thing that could possibly be changing the magnets is this square I keep standing in before I roll," she said, speaking quickly. "I'm willing to bet if I step in with my left foot first, meaning I apply pressure to the left side of the square, that the magnet behind the left wall moves into position. Or my right foot first, on the right side of the square, triggers the right wall magnet. Plus, for some reason, the magnets don't reset each time I step out of the square: That's why I just felt the pull of the left wall magnet when I held the ball near it."

Then she glared right into one of the cameras. (She had indeed spotted it!)

"If I jump and land with both feet at the same time," she told the poorly hidden camera, "I will have applied the same amount of pressure to both the left and right sides at the same time." She smiled and started laughing. "Which means BOTH magnets should move into place. And that means this ball will roll perfectly straight!"

Cynthia did what she had just finished explaining to the camera.

It was going straight: Directly for the hole.

And kept going straight.

Plunk!

In the hole!

"Bingo!" she exclaimed, watching a door swing open on the far side of the chamber.

She sprinted toward the open door, just in case there was some type of timing mechanism that would close it if she didn't enter within a specified number of seconds.

* * *

"She's almost in! She's almost in!" Neil said eagerly, eyes glued to the monitor.

Nicola was watching the screen as well, likely because she saw how close they were to succeeding in their mission.

Gabriella was quickly making her way to the chamber, as she had a vital duty to perform.

Cynthia darted through the opening, but paused once inside. (It was fairly dark, so she needed to fish a light out of her bag.)

Slam!

Gabriella had just closed the door of the trap! (Cynthia had walked right into one of their weather-god-proof boxes: Their plan had worked!)

Gabriella quickly started typing a message on her communicator: *Got Cyn!*

CHAPTER 38

Theo had just finished announcing the good news about Cynthia's capture when the red light on their monitor began flashing.

"Someone's coming, someone's coming," Claire said, pointing at the light. "But... there's only *one* person. Looks like a female, but it's a little hard to tell."

"I have a feeling I know who it is," Bradley said, approaching the TV to get a closer look. "If Cynthia was sent over there, we can pretty much count on this being Aurora."

"I see you share in my hatred of her," Theo commented. "But I can understand Xavier's decision to send her. She is one of his cleverest."

"Actually," Claire mentioned, "Brad's not worried about her powers or anything like that. You see, he used to have the hots for her. Well, until he figured out she was playing him for a fool."

Bradley's eyes darted at Claire. "You are the

last person who should be making comments like that," he said sharply. (But then he realized, immediately, that he should have kept his mouth shut...)

"Would you mind your own business for once?" she snapped at Bradley. "You think just because you got Neil and I back together once, that we owe it to you to stay together forever?"

"How am I supposed to respond to that?" Bradley replied angrily, with no intention of backing down here.

"Whatever," she said, facing her palm at Bradley and walking away.

Theo decided to intervene. "If you two want to argue about irrelevant matters," he said like he was preaching to them, "I can't stop you. But please hold off until we have Aurora in that box."

"I'm fine with that plan," Claire said, making sure she was the first to reply. "Brad's the one with the problem, not me."

Bradley scowled at Claire. "I'm fine, too," he told Theo. "But good luck getting her to keep her mouth shut."

* * *

Aurora let out a bit of a laugh while entering the cave: She was entertained to see that Mr. Winchester and Zoltan had set up a water cooler—exactly like the ones found in most company lunchrooms or doctor's office waiting rooms—just inside the entrance.

"Suppose I'll have a drink before getting started," she whistled while filling up one of the disposable paper cups. "This might just be the first thing they have ever done right."

She put the drink back in three big gulps, refilled her cup, and glugged the next one down quickly too.

"Much better," she smiled. "Now let's see what Leonardo and his band of misfits have in store for me." She laughed at her own comment. (She was truly loving every minute of this!)

Aurora was not particularly impressed by this challenge, which was no doubt a deterrent set up to foil whoever came in search of the amulet.

A small folding table, not much bigger than a student's desk, had been placed just inside the door. There were fifteen shiny metal blocks on the table, lined up in three neat rows of five. Each block was roughly the size of a golf ball, but no two were the same shape.

There was also an envelope on the table, which in all likelihood, would explain how these blocks were to be used.

"How can they possibly think a puzzle will stop me?" she commented while picking up the note. "All their silly game will do is *slightly delay* me."

In search of the amulet??

Well, we'll have to see if you have the

brains to get to it!

In the middle of this large chamber, you'll see a waist-high pedestal. (You can't miss it, it's the only thing in the middle of the room!) The surface of the pedestal is a very sensitive scale.

And I suppose the rest of the instructions are pretty simple.

To get the door on the opposite side of this room to open, you must place the correct block on the pedestal. And by the correct block, I mean the LIGHTEST block.

You may make three attempts. After your third attempt, the mechanism which allows the door to unlock will be severed, keeping the amulet behind this strong door for eternity.

"Who writes this garbage?" Aurora commented, shaking her head. "Is this supposed to make me shake in my boots?"

* * *

Bradley was seething. The sight of Aurora had pushed his irritation meter to *max.* He was also still peeved at Claire.

* * *

After examining the pedestal for a minute or two, Aurora walked back to the table with the blocks on it. She picked up the six-sided one and the pyramid-shaped one.

"The pyramid feels heavier," she said while comparing the two blocks by resting one on each palm. "I suppose I have no better way to do this. But as long as I am careful while comparing, I will eventually figure out which is the lightest."

She sighed at the boring task that she now had to begin.

"Anyway, I guess Zoltan and his gang lack the intelligence to come up with anything more academically challenging," she commented.

* * *

About fifteen minutes later, Aurora was reasonably confident that she had narrowed down six "candidates" for the lightest block. But the difference in weights was so minuscule that she started to second-guess herself. (She had experimented by switching the blocks between hands with her eyes closed, but that had only left her more undecided.)

She opted to go for the triacontagon (30-sided shape) on her first try. This one had so many sides on it that it almost looked like a sphere.

She gingerly put it down on the pedestal. At first, nothing happened. (Nothing ever happens at first, does it?)

But then the circular area in the center began slowly sinking. When it stopped, it was about two centimeters lower than its original position.

"Hey, door!" she yelled in the direction of the not-yet-open door. "Open already!"

* * *

"Idiot," Bradley happily mocked Aurora under his breath while watching all this on the TV monitors. "That was the fifth heaviest block. But you are too dumb to have even noticed."

Claire gravitated over to the monitors as well, but this time she (thankfully) chose to watch in silence.

* * *

Since the door clearly wasn't opening, Aurora picked up the 30-sided block—the one she thought should have worked—and hucked it at the exit. The metal hitting against rock made a sharp and uncomfortable noise.

Then Aurora tried to shake off some of her frustration—a technique all weather gods are trained in—as she knew a calm mind would translate to more effective contemplating.

* * *

Back at the table again, she returned to her efforts of comparing the various blocks. Not wanting to make another mistake, she elected to start again from scratch, rechecking all fourteen.

* * *

She was only able to eliminate four of the

fourteen blocks, as they were the only ones that were much heavier than the rest. But the other ten seemed so close in weight that she kept flipping back and forth about which ones to keep.

"I only get two more shots at this," she said, completely focused. "I must make them count. Being outsmarted by that brat Peter is not an option."

* * *

"Definitely not an option," Bradley laughed from his seat in front of the monitors. "It's more like *a guarantee.*"

* * *

One thing that was causing Aurora to be tricked was that every block had a different number of sides, thus causing the surface areas to be unequal. So when she put one of the blocks with fewer sides—such as the pyramid or cube—on her hand, a greater percentage of its overall surface area was touching her palm. (Comparing the blocks was turning into a huge headache!)

She then came up with a brilliant idea of how to nullify this: Instead of placing the blocks directly on her hands, she put a few crushed up tissues between her palms and the blocks.

"Much easier to tell now," she smiled.

* * *

It took some time, but she was able to eliminate four more.

"It's one of these six," she quietly said. "And since I have two more attempts, that translates to a one-in-three chance of guessing correctly. But that's not nearly good enough odds."

* * *

Five minutes later, she had eliminated one more.

* * *

And five minutes past that, another one.

"Only four left," she whispered to herself. (Why was she whispering?) "Now my odds are fifty-fifty."

Although she didn't love these odds, she felt they were good enough to use her second attempt. She went for the decagon (10-sided block) and was quite confident it was going to work.

After carefully placing it on the pedestal, the little platform began descending very slowly. (Noticeably slower than the first block she had tried.)

"I believe we have a winner!" she said proudly, strolling over to the door even before it began to open.

Nothing.

In a rage, she grabbed the decagon and threw it toward the entrance. It smashed into the wall just left of the water cooler, causing some pebbles to break off the wall. (She certainly didn't have any respect for ancient ruins or civilizations!)

Her high level of agitation quickly made her thirsty, so she made a beeline for the cooler. She removed a paper cup from the dispenser on the side and started filling it up.

But she was so preoccupied trying to sort out what to do next that she didn't realize her cup was overflowing.

She cursed (in Sevlarian) and then chugged back the cold water.

Now Aurora was glaring at the blocks, almost as if she was trying to scare these inanimate objects into telling her which was the correct one... But then something *incredible* came to her.

She started giggling.

Then chuckling.

Then roaring with laughter!

"I suppose I should give them a tiny bit of credit," she said while turning to face the water cooler. "They did make me use my noggin' a little."

HI READER! (^_^)
AURORA SEEMS TO HAVE FIGURED OUT WHAT TO DO!
HOW ABOUT YOU? ANY IDEA HOW SHE CAN

SOLVE THIS?

* * *

A few minutes later, Aurora had completed the task she had just set out to do: She had put water in thirteen paper cups, exactly the number of blocks left on the table. And she carefully made sure they all contained the same amount of water. So now she had 13 cups, each two-thirds full. And 13 blocks.

HI AGAIN, READER! (^_^)
SURELY YOU CAN GUESS WHAT SHE PLANS TO DO NEXT?

She started with the blocks she had previously decided as definitely being too heavy. She slowly put them in separate cups, one by one, making sure there was no splash. And what happened as each block went in?? It displaced the water, making the water level in the cup rise until some overflowed.

"Just as I thought!" she exclaimed. "I'm a genius!"

* * *

Finally, she eagerly moved on to the final three blocks, one of which had to be the *winner.*

"Since the blocks are all composed of the same material," she said in a cocky and arrogant tone, "that means whichever one has the smallest volume will displace the least water."

There was a heptagon (7 sides), a nonagon (9 sides), and a dodecagon (12 sides).

None of these three caused any water to overflow. And once fully submerged, it was clear which one was the lightest.

"Hello Mr. nonagon," she said, noticing that the surface of the water was more than a millimeter lower than the other two. "Shall we?"

Without skipping a beat, she grabbed the nonagon and placed it on the pedestal. The platform in the center lowered at an excruciatingly slow pace. And once it stopped, she heard a loud *click*. The stone door slowly began opening!

She rubbed her hands together while walking toward the goal.

"It's over!" she gloated. "The amulet is finally ours!"

But as soon as she was two or three steps into the dark (chamber? hallway? room?), she heard something behind her. Before she had a chance to spin around, something quickly closed and locked.

She had been tricked! And trapped!

CHAPTER 39

Maximillian proudly strolled through the tunnel, eager to get his hands on the prize. (Little did he know that a second—and even more confusing—puzzle was awaiting him!)

"Wha...?" he said in shock as he entered the chamber at the end of the tunnel. This enormous room contained a puzzle that looked both simple and terrifying at the same time.

Maximillian was now standing on a ledge that dropped off into a deep pit. And the far ledge—where the exit door lay—looked to be at least twenty meters from where he was currently standing.

The pit wasn't one giant, empty chasm. Instead, it looked more like a series of three chasms, one after another. So from Maximillian's current position, there were what looked like two narrow "ridges"—one which was one-third the way across, and the other two-thirds the way across—between him and the far side. But the way to get to each ridge, and ultimately the far side, looked daunting...

There were nine very old-looking rope bridges. And the configuration of these bridges was completely baffling.

To get to the first ridge, there was only one bridge, which had been labeled with a large yellow *1.*

From the first ridge to the second ridge, there were three bridges, numbered *2, 3,* and *4.*

And from the second ridge to the far side, there were five bridges, labeled *5, 6, 7, 8,* and *9.*

Maximillian looked at the envelope laying on the ground just in front of the first rope bridge, which he was fairly sure would contain a riddle he needed to solve to unveil the correct route across. But before picking it up, he gingerly put the toe of his right shoe on the first bridge, plus he shook its ropes with his hands. These bridges had probably been sturdy centuries ago, but now some of the boards looked rotten, and others had fallen away.

His nervousness had caused his pulse to quicken a little when he had a sudden revelation.

"What am I worried about?" he laughed. "I can just fly my way across."

He prepared to conjure up a small cyclone to carry himself over: something that usually required almost no effort.

But his powers were not working! Not at all!

"There must be something about this area of the caves that renders my powers useless," he said in frustration. "Could have something to do with the composition of the rocks down here. Anyhow, I don't need my powers to do this, I easily have enough brains."

He removed the note from the envelope, ready for a sarcastic and taunting message.

Numbers, numbers, numbers... who doesn't love them?

Your way across involves nothing more than simply adding things up!

Here is your clue:

FOUR
FIVE
TWELVE

Good Luck!

P.S. Choose carefully! You only get one attempt at this!

"Four, five, twelve?" Maximillian said aloud, looking at the rickety bridges. "But the numbered bridges only go up to nine!"

* * *

Peter and his team had a bird's eye view of the chamber. They were standing in a compartment that was directly above the exit door, looking out through small holes that had been drilled in the walls.

"I say it takes him at least an hour," Peter whispered to Bridget and Torin. "Anyone wanna bet me five bucks?"

"You're on," Bridget whispered back. "Max is a genius. He won't need an hour."

"I think I'll just observe," Torin commented. "I don't have any Earth money, anyway. If I lost, I wouldn't be able to pay up."

* * *

"Math certainly comes into play here," Maximillian said to himself, eyes scanning the note carefully. "Well, for starters, there is only one bridge to the first ridge, and it has a big *1* on it. The difference between the first two numbers in the clue, 4 and 5, is 1. Hmm…"

Seasoned puzzlers like Maximillian knew the thought process required when considering various possibilities, but they also understood how difficult *only-one-attempt* puzzles were. (Those were, in most cases, the worst type!)

He got out a paper and pen, so he could write a few notes. (Another sign that he was a veteran problem-solver.)

4 and 5 (difference of 1)

5 and 12 (difference of 7)

4 and 12 (difference of 8)

"No, that doesn't help me," he said, relatively calmly. "I need a *2, 3,* or *4* to get from the first ridge to the second one."

* * *

Peter couldn't dismiss his extreme interest in watching Maximillian tackle this conundrum. (Maximillian was pacing around and mumbling, exactly what Peter did when he tried to solve puzzles!)

Weirdly, Peter was kind of rooting for this evil weather god. As satisfying as it would be to say he had stumped Maximillian, it would be equally rewarding to see the look on the face of anyone who could solve it. (Peter, stop cheering for the bad guy!)

* * *

"Back to the drawing board," Maximillian grumbled, pulling out a fresh sheet of paper.

4 + 5 = 9 (add 1 to get 10)

5 + 12 = 17 (add 3 to get 20)

4 + 12 = 16 (add 4—

"Nope," he said a little less patiently than before. "I'm missing something here... The clue mentioned adding, right?" he asked himself. "But what am I supposed to add to what?"

Maximillian sat down and dangled his legs over the ledge. This riddle was turning out to be harder than he wanted to admit.

* * *

A little over five minutes later (Peter had been timing him, of course!), Maximillian took out a third sheet of paper and wrote a very simple list.

1
2
3
4
5
6
7
8
9

He looked back and forth between his paper and the clue, over and over again.

"Now this may be grasping at straws," he said, "but it does seem a little peculiar that the numbers in the clue were written as words instead of digits."

To confirm that this was strictly a coincidence, he wrote out the words beside the numbers.

1   *one*
2   *two*
3   *three*
4   *four*
5   *five*
6   *six*
7   *seven*
8   *eight*
9   *nine*

"What's hiding under the surface here?" he said inquisitively. "1 + 1 is 2, right? 1 + *one* is… wait!" He smiled. (A big, victorious smile!)

HI READER!
MAXIMILLIAN JUST HAD A BRAINWAVE!
ANY IDEA WHAT HE MAY HAVE SPOTTED?

"The word *one* has three letters in it!" he cheered prematurely. "If I take the digit *1,* add it the number of the letters in the word *one,* which is 3, I get 4. Yes, FOUR!"

He quickly jotted down the rest of these calculations on his paper.

1 + one (3 letters) = FOUR
2 + two (3 letters) = FIVE
3 + three (5 letters) = EIGHT
4 + four (4 letters) = EIGHT

5 + five (4 letters) = NINE
6 + six (3 letters) = NINE
7 + seven (5 letters) = TWELVE
8 + eight (5 letters) = THIRTEEN
9 + nine (4 letters) = THIRTEEN

"Eureka!" he exclaimed, eyes focused on the right side of his list, specifically on the *FOUR, FIVE,* and *TWELVE.* He then copied the three equations he needed to solve this puzzle.

1 + one (3 letters) = FOUR
2 + two (3 letters) = FIVE
7 + seven (5 letters) = TWELVE

"FOUR corresponds to the *1,* which is my first bridge," he said excitedly. *"FIVE* means the bridge with the *2* on it. And the *TWELVE* is the bridge with the *7."*

He took the original note and all three papers he had written on, crushed them into a tight ball, and hurled it as far as he could.

* * *

"Is that the answer?" Bridget asked Peter. "Did he just figure it out?"

Peter smiled. (You'll just have to wait and see!)

Regardless of how flimsy the bridges looked, Maximillian walked across them as if they were strong enough to support an elephant.

"That was almost fun!" he laughed as he

stepped off the final bridge and onto the far ledge after walking across the *1, 2,* and *7.* But right before going through the exit, he paused...

CHAPTER 40

Torin was now in place to shut the door of the trap as soon as Maximillian walked in. But the evil weather god seemed to have caught on to what was happening! (This was something they hadn't prepared for...)

Now what?

Peter and Bridget looked at each other, but neither had any idea what to do next.

"Something's not right," Maximillian said, starting to turn around.

Before he had twisted the full 180 degrees, Torin, who was full out sprinting, grabbed Maximillian and tackled him like a linebacker did to the opposing team's star quarterback.

The force took them both tumbling into the special box.

Torin was neither athletic nor strong, but he was doing whatever he could to hold Maximillian down.

"Peter! Close it! Hurry!" Torin yelled.

Maximillian hit Torin with a hard left hook and quickly got the upper hand. He followed that with an elbow to the kidney. Then he stood up.

Slam!

Peter got the door shut and locked in time.

So they now had Max! (But Torin was in there, too...)

CHAPTER 41

The physical struggle between Maximillian and Torin continued despite the complete darkness of the box they were trapped in.

"You'll pay for this!" Maximillian screamed while thrashing around at Torin. "You'll pay with your life!"

Torin was using every bit of energy he had to defend himself, so he didn't bother responding.

But Torin's relative weakness compared to the bigger, stronger, and fitter Maximillian meant he didn't stand a chance. Before he knew it, the evil weather god had him pinned to the floor.

"Peter!" Maximillian yelled. "If you want your friend here to live, open this box! Immediately!"

"Don't do it, Peter!" Torin screamed. "Whatever you do, do NOT let him out!"

Peter was torn. His instincts told him he had to save his friend. (So yes, he had to open it!)

But wait, Torin had just explicitly told him not to open the box. (So he shouldn't open it...)

"Pete," Bridget advised him. "We can't let Torin die. No way. Max has no powers down here. If we open the box, he'll have to fight us three on one, with his bare hands. We can take him down."

"No! Peter! No!" Torin tried yelling. "It's too risky! Don't—"

Smack!

Maximillian had just belted Torin hard in the stomach.

Ring-ring

"Huh?" Peter said, looking around to see where this noise was coming from.

Ring-ring

"What do you think that is?" Peter asked Bridget.

"No clue," she replied. "But it sounds like it's coming from your backpack."

"My backpack?" Peter said, fumbling to take it off and quickly unzipping it.

She was right. There was some sort of device in his backpack. It was a small rectangular screen, about 10 centimeters by 6 centimeters in size. And the face being displayed on the screen was one he knew all too well... Xavier!

Below the screen, there was a small button, labeled *answer.*

"Torin!" Peter yelled in a panic before answering. "It's Xavier! What should I do?"

Torin was, unfortunately, in no condition to reply.

"Looks like the cavalry has arrived!" Maximillian cheered. "That means you all lose!"

Peter pushed the button and held the screen close to his face. "We aren't afraid of you!" Peter said loudly to Xavier.

"Oh, please," Xavier laughed, mocking Peter. "Even you can see I have the upper hand."

"No, you don't," Peter said with fake confidence. "We have just trapped Aurora, Cynthia, and Maximillian. If you don't believe—"

"I already know that," Xavier barked at Peter.

Peter wasn't about to give the evilest of the evil any breathing room, so he quickly threw out a threat.

"If you want them back alive," Peter instructed Xavier, "then call off your invasion, and leave the people of Earth alone. Forever."

Xavier's laugh grew louder and deeper: He was not intimidated in the least.

"Go ahead and kill all three, for all I care," he remarked. "They are completely expendable."

"Expendable?" Maximillian said from the box, having heard Xavier's last comment.

Xavier laughed even louder. "Those three have

been nothing more than just stupid guinea pigs," he remarked. "I am glad to rid of them."

"I'm calling your bluff," Peter said back right away.

"Look," Xavier said, rolling his eyes. "I've known since earlier today that this was all a trap. I could have contacted them before they landed on Earth, and told them not to proceed. But I wanted to see what you and your crew had cooked up for them."

"What are you...?" Peter said, completely confused. "How?"

"Enough meaningless banter," Xavier said coldly. "Now it's my turn to present you with an ultimatum: Hand over the amulet, or we will kill anyone and everyone who stands in our way."

"Never!" Torin screamed from the box. "You'll never—"

"Silence!" Xavier yelled.

"Peter," Xavier went on. "By keeping the amulet, you will be the one responsible for the deaths of many, many people... But I suppose that's not such a big thing, is it? Because you'll be dead, too!"

Click

Xavier had cut the connection.

"Now what do you think of that leader of yours?" Torin asked Maximillian, expecting to be punched for his remark. "He could have saved you from all of this, but he chose not to!"

Maximillian softened his grip on Torin.

"All he cares about is himself," Torin told Maximillian. "No one else means anything to him. Can't you see that?"

There was a long pause.

"Peter," Torin eventually said. "Let us both out."

Peter didn't reply at first. He looked at Bridget, who shrugged her shoulders.

"Umm... okay," he said, opening the box.

Maximillian had fire in his eyes. "Xavier must pay for this," he said with conviction. "Aurora, Cynthia, and I will do anything we can to help defend against his invasion. I only ask for one thing: Let me be the one to finish off Xavier."

"I am afraid you'll have to stand in line to do that," Peter said with a smirk, shaking Maximillian's cold and sweaty hand. "There is a long list of people who want to get at him first."

Thank you for reading *Enormously Puzzled.* I hope you liked all the adventure, plot twists, and (of course!) the bizarre, head-scratching puzzles! If you enjoyed this book, it would be super-duper if you took a minute to review it on Amazon or Goodreads. Thank you so much!

And please don't hesitate to contact me (pj@pjnichols.com) if you have any comments or questions. The wonderful emails I've received are heartwarming, and your suggestions have been tremendous – your advice has helped me so much when deciding what will happen next in Peter's adventure! And if you haven't tried the puzzles on my website (pjnichols.com) yet, check it out and put your problem-solving skills to the test!

Sincerely,

P.J. Nichols

Acknowledgements

To each and every science teacher I had while growing up, who patiently listened to my countless "Why?" questions, and then explained the reasons (in detail) until I was satisfied. My interest in science has never waned, and I'll do what I can to conjure up some more science-related puzzles to include in the rest of the series.

To the staff of the little café near my home—the place where I do most of my writing—who are welcoming and pleasant every single day, even though all I ever buy is two cups of coffee. If it hadn't been for your quiet and comfortable shop, I would still be back on Book 2 or 3...

To the wonderful people who do random acts of kindness for others. If we all did one nice thing for someone every day, imagine how happy the world would be!

To all the readers, both young and old (and middle-aged, too!) It brings me an inexplicable amount of happiness to know you are enjoying the stories as much as I loved writing them!

About the Author

"How do you come up with all the puzzles??"

This is a question PJ receives quite regularly, so he's going to try his best to explain how he does this (without writing a 5-page essay on it!)

Many of the puzzles and riddles are formed/imagined while PJ is out on one of his morning "power-walks." The process he usually follows goes something like this:

1. Look at something (a mailbox, a fire hydrant, etc.) or think of something (the law of gravity, a key, etc.)
2. List off everything you know about it. (This is the relatively easy part.)
3. (Now for the hard part!) Try imagining how (or if?) you could use it in a puzzle or riddle.
4. If nothing comes to mind quickly during "step 3," then return to "step 1" and pick something different.

And as crazy as this may sound, PJ thoroughly enjoys every minute of this, as it really gets his mind moving!

Visit P.J. at www.pjnichols.com

CPSIA information can be obtained
at www.ICGtesting.com
Printed in the USA
LVHW100310081222
734689LV00006B/455